Readers love the Shifter Hardball
series by CHEYENNE MEADOWS

Friends With Benefits

"Overall this is a lovely book, with a catchy storyline."
—Sinfully: Gay Romance Book Reviews

"The well written scenes and details draw the reader in to the story,
while the perfect blend of fun, serious and passion-filled scenes
ensures that the reader enjoys every last page of this romance."
—The Romance Reviews

Loaded for Bear

"The sexy times are hot, the men are macho with a soft, gooey
inside, and the story entertaining—not a bad combination."
—The Novel Approach

"This story is written with love and dedication and I saw and felt it
all the way though."
—GGR Reviews

"This was an amazing read and I cannot wait for the next book in the
series to come out and see what this team gets up to next."
—Inked Rainbow Reads

By CHEYENNE MEADOWS

Feline Persuasion
Relentless
Shadowing Mace

SHIFTER HARDBALL
Friends With Benefits
Loaded for Bear
Switch Hitter

Published by DREAMSPINNER PRESS
www.dreamspinnerpress.com

SWITCH
Hitter
CHEYENNE MEADOWS

DREAMSPINNER PRESS

Published by
DREAMSPINNER PRESS

5032 Capital Circle SW, Suite 2, PMB# 279, Tallahassee, FL 32305-7886 USA
www.dreamspinnerpress.com

This is a work of fiction. Names, characters, places, and incidents either are the product of author imagination or are used fictitiously, and any resemblance to actual persons, living or dead, business establishments, events, or locales is entirely coincidental.

Switch Hitter
© 2017 Cheyenne Meadows.

Cover Art
© 2017 Reese Dante.
http://www.reesedante.com
Cover content is for illustrative purposes only and any person depicted on the cover is a model.

ISBN: 978-1-63533-586-6
Digital ISBN: 978-1-63533-587-3
Library of Congress Control Number: 2017901552
Published June 2017
v. 1.0

Printed in the United States of America
∞
This paper meets the requirements of
ANSI/NISO Z39.48-1992 (Permanence of Paper).

Chapter 1

CRACK.

Dixon watched as one of his teammates darted for home, gracefully sliding across the plate even though the throw wasn't even close. *Tucker. Tucker Wilde.* The wild dog shifter who played second base for their team and the object of Dixon's wet dreams for the past few months.

Tucker stood, not bothering to dust himself off, and retrieved the discarded bat lying nearby. When he bent over, his lily-white rear shone through a long L-shaped tear in his uniform pants.

Dixon chuckled as Tucker tilted his head and then patted his posterior, obviously feeling a bit of a breeze on his backside.

"Nice rip," Wiley, the shortstop, hollered. "You might want to cover it up, though."

"And soon," Trigger, the cranky catcher, added with a good dose of command.

While Dixon agreed on the compliment, he wasn't in as much of a hurry to see that small portion out of sight.

Tucker trotted toward the bench, pausing at the steps leading down into the dugout area. "Why do I have a feeling that my butt is going to be plastered all over the sports channels for the next two days?" He shook his head and grinned at Dixon.

"Probably because it is?"

Even as they spoke, a cameraman hustled behind Tucker, lowered the angle of his camera, and fixated on Tucker's rump.

"There's already enough bad shit on television. Do we really have to add Tucker's bare ass to it?" Trigger growled at the media guy. The man looked up, blinked, and made a hasty retreat.

"Hey, grizzly. Some people might like to see a little peekaboo from me." Tucker wiggled his rear before turning to face Trigger, which ended up giving Dixon a great view of the flapping opening in the pants.

"Yeah, right. Keep wishing." Trigger plopped down on the bench and snarled at Tucker.

2

Tucker was one of a kind and well-liked. If the players took a vote, Tucker would surely be a leading candidate for team clown.

Although, in this situation, Dixon wasn't sure his silly antics hadn't gotten Tucker in over his head.

Unable to resist, Dixon rolled his eyes, then laughed. "You're cruising for a bruising, buddy. Better think about changing before Trigger gets serious."

Tucker flashed him a mischievous grin. "What fun is it if you don't poke the grizzly a little?"

"Fun or suicidal?" Dixon asked.

Trigger stared intently at Tucker as if daring him to press his luck. Dixon had seen that look in the past—right before Trigger launched into pissed-off bear mode.

"Just because he's happily mated doesn't mean he's mellowed, Tucker," Dixon warned. The polar bear shifter, Graham, seemed to be the only person who had the ability to chill Trigger out. Too bad, as a pitcher, Graham was relegated to the bull pen for the moment.

"Whatcha going to do, bear? Huh? Cat got your tongue?" Tucker teased while shaking his butt at Trigger again.

In a flash, Trigger lurched toward Tucker with a menacing growl.

Tucker scurried out of reach just in the nick of time. The playful threat didn't stop him from flipping Trigger the bird along with a mischievous grin. *Egging it on. Like usual.*

The other players in the dugout broke out in laughter at the antics. Dixon included.

Trigger grinned wolfishly. "Good thing I actually sorta, maybe, almost like you."

Tucker's mouth fell open at the admission.

"Go change already. It's not like the whole game is going to stop because you're hanging out to dry." Banner, the manager, waved toward the door leading to the locker room. His ordering tone ceased the fun. For now.

Tucker saluted and quickly disappeared.

Dixon tried not to stare at the flexing of firm muscles exposed for his viewing pleasure. When the door shut, Dixon turned his attention back to the game.

In the process, he noticed Wiley looking at him with what could only be called a Cheshire cat grin on his face. "What?"

Wiley shook his head but didn't answer otherwise. The smile remained as well.

Well, hell. Wiley obviously caught his interest in Tucker's partially covered rear. Nothing new, per se, since the whole team knew he was gay. However, he could see Wiley rattling his cage a bit about checking out a teammate for more than the size of bat he carried. The wolf shifter had a devilish streak that popped out now and again. Dixon would just have to wait patiently to see if anything came of his enthrallment with Tucker's ass.

Smack.

The line drive flew just over the dugout, causing the guys standing at the rail to duck in a hurry.

"That had some heat on it."

Dixon heard the familiar male voice and turned to find Tucker emerging from the locker room with a towel loosely hanging from around his neck. Sweat dripped from the sides of the wild dog's face and onto his baseball uniform, leaving it soaked in places. The fresh pair of bright, clean white pants contrasted with the dirty shirt.

And covered up Tucker's previously exposed rear. *Damn it.*

Actually, it was for the best. Dixon didn't mind the eye candy but preferred to avoid riding the bench with a hard-on. Cups and erections didn't fit together comfortably.

"Why didn't you put on a fresh jersey too?"

"It would just get dirty."

Dixon blinked at the rationalization. "So?"

Tucker shrugged. "So, the one I'm wearing is already dirty. Might as well save on the laundry bill when possible."

"Okay." Dixon shook his head in amusement. Not like the team pinched pennies, and all the players could certainly afford a few luxuries. Their large salaries guaranteed that. Leave it to Tucker to notice the small things and buck what others would typically do in the process.

"It's as hot as hell today." Tucker wiped at the beads of moisture once again.

4

Dixon could empathize. Though it was only preseason, the high nineties temperature made them all perspire and droop. Preston, their home city, was normally a good fifteen degrees cooler this time of year. Unfortunately, an early taste of summer had arrived, nearly before spring officially set in.

"Better keep your head on a stick around here. Those rookies can hit." Dixon leaned back and stretched his arms out on the backrest of the bench.

Tucker nodded and sat down beside him. "They have promise." He wiped his brow with the towel. "Most of them anyway."

Dixon watched as one of the new guys on the team took his place in the batter's box. Ares. Ares Warr. An unusual name for an unusual guy. One of the very few hybrid shifters in the league. A wolf-dingo cross at that. Dixon wasn't sure what that meant in the scheme of things, but the kid had talent. Tons of it.

Since this was the last preseason game, Banner, the manager, decided to put all the rookies on the roster, replacing several of the starters for this one game. Dixon sat this one out while Ares took his spot. Tucker, on the other hand, had been at his usual second base position for most of the game. He'd just been relieved a few minutes ago. Thus, the accumulation of dust, dirt, and sweat.

"What do you think of Lance?" Lance, the top draft pick of the Preston Predators, also happened to be a tiger shifter.

Tucker shrugged. "Time will tell." Tucker grabbed a bottle of water from a nearby cooler, removed the cap, and chugged half the liquid down.

The bobbing of his Adam's apple snared Dixon's attention and drew his mind off the topic of baseball and to his ever-present simmering libido.

Dixon secretly grinned at the walking mess Tucker presented. He'd been in the dirt to catch balls as well as sliding into bases. While others might be hesitant to get close and risk getting smudged or catching a whiff of sweat, Dixon didn't mind in the least. More than that, he found the combination downright sexy.

Tucker could only be called a looker. The quintessential tall, dark, and handsome guy mixed those physical attributes with a healthy sense of humor, a wicked grin, and chocolate eyes that flashed mischief nearly as much as intelligence. He had muscles galore, but not so bulky that he'd lose speed. More like just a big guy with a nicely filled-out frame. Wide chest, narrower waist, powerful thighs, and a perfectly rounded ass. Throw him into a uniform and he made quite the showstopper. Scuffed up from playing baseball only made him more appealing in Dixon's opinion. Not that he'd verbalized that fact. No way.

Because Tucker was straight. Always had been as far as Dixon knew. Most likely always would be too.

"Bringing that girl of yours to the party tomorrow night?" Dixon studied Tucker, waiting patiently for the all-important answer.

Tucker replaced the cap on the bottle, then rested his hands in his lap. "Yeah. She can't wait to see the extravagance of that estate. Been talking about it for a couple of weeks." Neil Garrison owned the Preston Predators. He'd opened his mansion to all the players and other high society members in an annual get-together.

Dixon sighed in resignation. He'd hoped and dreamed since Tucker joined the team. All to no avail. Now, he'd pretty much given up on the belief that they could ever be more than friends and teammates. While Tucker might be a switch hitter in the game of baseball, he didn't seem to be in his social life. Which was too damn bad, in Dixon's opinion.

"Bringing someone along for the party?" Tucker asked.

"No." Dixon turned his attention back to the field.

"Why not?"

"I haven't found anyone that suited, I guess."

Tucker scooted a smidge closer and gestured toward Ares playing third base. "What about him? He's put together well. A canine, to boot."

Dixon rolled his eyes. "You know how wolves are, even mixtures. Besides, he's a rookie. Could be traded in a couple of weeks." The problem with early season was that rosters weren't finalized for a couple months or so after opening day. Jostling and trades were a given during this time of year and made for some chaotic times. Especially for new players.

"True." Tucker grinned. "I'd say you and Trigger would make a great match if not for Graham beating you to him."

6

Dixon snorted. "Are you trying to get me killed?" The only two bears on the team paired up last season. Trigger had a soft spot for Graham. He treated the rest of the guys like his hired servants. Dixon didn't take it personally. Trigger pretty much ran the show, was the best catcher in the league, and helped the team pull off the coveted series finale trophy last year. For that, he'd put up with playing with the devil himself and sustain a few harsh corrections aimed his way.

"Well...." Tucker chuckled before taking another drink. "Seriously, though. It's time you hook up with a bedmate."

"I do okay on my own." The thought of Tucker helping him find a man seemed a bit ironic if not totally crazy.

"Says the man without a date for the big party." Tucker tossed the empty bottle into a nearby trash can. "Tell me what you're looking for in a guy and I'll help you find one."

Dixon arched an eyebrow. "You're going to help me pick out a guy?" He'd always been gay and everyone on the team knew it. Thankfully, the Preston Predators embraced everyone, including mated pairs among the gay players. If another team dared throw insults that revolved around sexual orientation, Dixon knew his teammates would have his back. Hell, he'd been part of the pack at the end of last season when Graham's old team started some bullshit. The Predators shut them down real fast. Not just in standing up to them, but in beating them for the championship too.

"Yep." Tucker smiled even more. "What? Just because my gate swings the other way, you don't think I can tell a sex-on-a-stick guy from a dumpster dive?"

Dixon reluctantly grinned. "Good point."

"See. Let me think. The guy has to have a great ass. After all, that's the part you're checking out all the time, right?"

You certainly have a nice one. Dixon groaned to himself and wiggled a bit in his seat for comfort. "Not *all* the time. Besides, it helps if the guy has other assets. A nice rear doesn't always make the man."

Tucker tapped his lips. "I hadn't thought much about it before, but I guess it's not that different from searching for a fine woman. Just less curves and more muscles." He paused for a second. "So, a guy with a great ass and a good-looking face. Top of the list."

"What about brains?"

Tucker blinked at him in confusion. "What about them?"

"Damn, Tucker. I want a man. Not a blow-up doll."

Tucker threw his head back and guffawed.

The sound rolled through Dixon, increasing his desire as well as easing his tension. He'd never tire of Tucker or his laughter, even if it was at his own expense.

A stiff breeze blew through the dugout, tousling Tucker's deep black hair, parting it enough to emphasize the blond spot about the size of a sticky note just above his left temple. A testament to Tucker's wild dog genetics and a mark Dixon considered cute. In Tucker's shifted form, numerous spots of yellow and white broke up the solid black base. He even sported a white tuft on the end of his tail. Something Dixon found amusing.

Overall, Tucker was a man in his prime, his shifter DNA adding to his strength and impression. He carried himself with self-confidence and a flair of regality. The dimples in his cheeks were as endearing as his sometimes off-the-wall sense of humor.

Tucker was a good guy. A sexy man. And a hell of a baseball player.

All the more reason Dixon wanted him.

Except Tucker didn't see Dixon in the same way. They did things as friends, sure, but Dixon never broached the subject of inviting Tucker into his bed. Too afraid of rejection to utter the words.

If I only had some sign that he tipped into the bi category....

But it had never happened. So, he admired Tucker from afar, so to say. Fantasizing about what could be, kept Dixon hot and bothered some nights. But, in the daytime, reality took over, placing him back into the role of friend and nothing more.

"Don't you know how much fun blow-up dolls are?" Tucker waggled his eyebrows.

Dixon elbowed him. "I don't have a thing for plastic. Thank you, very much."

"Picky, picky."

"Yep."

Tucker glanced from Dixon and back to the field. "Does he have to be canine? A shifter?"

"I haven't gotten that far."

Tucker turned back to stare at him. "What do you mean you haven't gotten that far?"

"Just what I said."

"Well, that's your problem right there. You just have to narrow your criteria down to what you want, then see who fits into that mold." Tucker nodded.

You'll fit. I'm sure of it.

Dixon rubbed his forehead. "Is this like your penchant for dating redheads?"

Tucker grinned widely. "Yep. I hunt... err, search for redheads, find one, then end up asking them out."

"And how's that working for you?" Dixon couldn't quite grasp Tucker's dating philosophy. The color of hair had little to do with the person, in his opinion.

"Found quite a few. They never disappoint. Especially this one. Gloria is damn hot in the sack, sexy as hell, and fun. That's how it's working out."

Frustrated with the topic at hand, Dixon remained mute. The last thing he wanted to hear about was Tucker's latest exploits in bed.

If she's so great, why haven't you put a ring on her finger?

Dixon already knew the answer to his unvoiced question. Tucker was a playboy. Had been as long as Dixon had known him. He dated redheads almost exclusively, kept them around for a while, until the women started seeing wedding dresses and baby carriages in Tucker's future. Then he retreated—fast. The tendency offered a blip of hope to Dixon about a future with Tucker, but nothing more.

Cheers drew his attention back to the game. Wiley stepped up to the plate, bunted the first pitch, and managed to beat the throw to first. His success ended up loading the bases in the favor of the Predators.

Dixon clapped in appreciation for the effort and outcome.

"What about Slade?"

Automatically, Dixon looked to the bull pen, his gaze landing on the tall jaguar shifter. As he watched, Slade wound up and threw the ball into the catcher's glove. Last season, an injury sat Slade on the sidelines for several months. Now, he was back. With something to prove if his pitching numbers meant anything.

While Dixon could appreciate the guy, he didn't feel the sparks or butterflies like he did when he hung out with Tucker. Not even close. "He's a good guy. Just doesn't do it for me."

"What about Mack?"

Dixon shook his head. "Nothing."

Tucker slapped him on the shoulder. "The way I see it, bro, is that you either need to jump in with both feet or invest in that blow-up doll."

"You're just too damn easy," Dixon threw back without menace.

"And you're too hard." Tucker smiled lopsidedly. His eyes twinkled with mirth. "Probably in all kinds of ways."

The teasing went straight to Dixon's needy cock. Not for the first time, he appreciated the looseness of the uniform even if the cup presently chafed his sensitive skin and compressed his genitals into what felt like a sardine can. "You're a mess." Dixon couldn't resist grinning.

"Not the worst I've been called." Tucker stood and headed to the steps to watch the game better.

Dixon couldn't take his eyes off Tucker's rear the entire time.

Now this is the life. Dixon chuckled to himself, relished the breeze, and enjoyed the scenery before him. The baseball diamond faded away as he stared at far more interesting things.

Good thing the game seized his undivided attention when he was on the field playing third base. Life on the hot corner could be dangerous at times.

So could cornering Tucker and spilling his feelings.

No sooner had the thought arrived than Dixon shut it down. The time wasn't right.

It'll never be right at this rate. Stop being a dumbass and just tell the guy. The inner voice belonging to his gray fox chastised him rarely, and always about his social life or lack thereof.

Dixon ignored it, just like he'd done before.

If it's meant to be, then it'll happen.

The phrase fell flat even in his own mind.

Chapter 2

TUCKER TOOK his normal position on second base for infield practice. Rain the night before left the usual dirt patches slick and muddy, although the temperature had cooled considerably, making the morning on the verge of chilly. Much better than the steamy tropical feeling of yesterday.

He hit his glove with his free hand, bent his knees, and shifted his weight. His focus latched onto the ball presently in Steve, the pitching coach's, hand. The guy normally threw batting practice, but helped in other ways as well.

A line drive had Tucker laying out toward the first base side. He hit the ground hard, sliding a couple of feet through a small mud puddle, and still came up empty-handed. Annoyed, he stood up, glanced down, and found himself damp from the ground and covered in the slippery substance. *What a wonderful way to start the day*, he grouched to himself.

"I hear wild dogs love mud," Dixon said from third base.

"Something about mud baths?" Wiley added.

Tucker snorted but didn't take offense. The nature of their relationship revolved around giving one another a hard time. "Are you talking about spas? Never been to one, but I understand wolves like to have their nails painted there while getting one of those goopy face treatments."

Wiley growled, then dove for a sharply hit baseball. He collected it and tossed it to Tucker, who automatically stepped on the bag before throwing a laser to Ram waiting at first.

Before Tucker could say anything more, a fly ball came his way. He backpedaled, adjusted, then reached out, only to have the ball bounce off the end of his glove. "Well, shit." He picked it up and threw it back to Banner who handed out the balls to Steve.

"Tucker. What's with you today?" Banner hollered across the field.

Tucker waved briefly with his glove. "Just getting good and awake."

Banner didn't say anything more, though he continued to feed balls to Steve.

The next one bounced toward Dixon. Dixon squared up just in time for the ball to take a large hop, right over his head. Dixon turned a full circle, obviously searching for it.

"Hey, Foxy. It's between your feet." Tucker chuckled at the bewildered expression on Dixon's face.

Dixon bent over, barehanded the ball, and threw it back in. Task complete, he flipped Tucker off.

"Yeah, yeah. Maybe it would help if you grew a little." Tucker couldn't resist yanking Dixon's chain. They were good friends from day one. He'd arrived at the team's facility not knowing a single person. Dixon made the first overture, welcomed him, and helped him settle into a new city. Since then, they were tight buddies on the field. Off, they tended to go their separate ways. Tucker somewhat regretted not hanging out with Dixon, but he had his hands full with the ladies and little free time to spare due to their relentless schedule during baseball season. He made a mental note that when the season ended, he should make a point of attending guys' night out with the rest of his buddies.

"This coming from the walking mud monster?" Dixon responded tartly. The twitching of his lips clued Tucker in that he was just throwing verbal crap right back rather than getting truly irritated.

"I might be covered in mud, but at least I can find the ball." Tucker lifted his chin and added a haughty quality to his voice.

"You're such a furball at times." Dixon shook his head while chuckling.

"Guys," Wiley said.

"Takes one to know one," Tucker retorted.

"Guys!" Wiley hollered.

Not to be dissuaded, Tucker walked toward Dixon and stopped. *There's a better way to show him a thing or three.* In the blink of an eye, he shifted into his wild dog form, shook off his uniform, found the mud puddle, and rolled.

"I thought we were practicing!" Ram yelled from first base.

Tucker ignored him, ran over to Dixon, stopped a few feet away, and shook. Water and small clumps of mud flew through the air, landing mostly on Dixon. Wiley, due to his shortstop position, caught a few as well.

"Oh, no. You didn't." Wiley growled, then quickly changed into his wolf form.

He took out after Tucker, but Tucker was too fast. His long legs gave him an advantage in speed, while Wiley's heavier form gave him the edge in strength and bulk. But not by much.

"Oh, hell. We'll never finish practice at this rate." Dixon crossed his arms and scowled at them.

Tucker changed direction and launched himself at Dixon. The force put Dixon on his ass. Tucker barked with laughter, grasped Dixon's glove in his strong jaws, then sped away. He didn't get too far before he glimpsed Dixon following suit, becoming his gray fox, and joining in the chase. The change from light brown hair to a light gray coat always surprised Tucker as most shifters carried the same coloring in both forms.

"Canines." Trigger spit out the word in disgust.

"Someone might as well throw them a ball already," Ram said.

"Here. Catch." Ares lobbed a baseball into the frenzy.

Ram snorted. "I think you meant *fetch*."

Ares grinned and shrugged, then morphed into his animal form, obviously not wanting to be left out of the fun. His dingo-wolf form sported a tall body with a thick coat just a couple of hues from being perfectly white. More like a hint of strawberry in the coloring. Tall and powerful, he seemed to be the epitome of both species. Tucker appreciated him even more after seeing his shifted form.

For a split second, Tucker wondered how Ares's family dealt with his hybrid genetics. Before he could consider it further, Dixon darted at his side, sharp white teeth shining as he moved to take back the glove.

Tucker evaded him, lifted the glove higher in the air, and took off toward right field, Dixon right on his heels.

"This is exactly why we need more bears on the team. You wouldn't catch any of us out there playing 'keep away.'" Trigger's voice carried easily to Tucker whose hearing became all that more advanced with the shift.

He glimpsed Banner rolling his eyes in reaction. "At least canines are halfway social and easy to deal with. Bears, on the other hand…."

"Are the best," Graham finished.

Tucker eavesdropped on the conversation, then hit full stride in order to dodge Wiley and barely avoid a collision with Ares. He turned to discover Dixon still right behind him and keeping up, despite his shorter legs and more compact frame.

That guy can run. Tucker gave credit where credit was due.

His animal side yipped in his mind, happy to be free at what had spontaneously turned into a dog park.

Dixon right on his tail only made the fun all that much better. One of the most laid-back players on the team, Dixon was as steady as he was talented. The guy didn't always let his hair down or his fox out to play. But when he did, it was on.

Tucker was just as thrilled as his inner beast. It'd been a long time since he'd run with friends. Never with pack mates. Now, he had the chance. For down deep he considered the team his family. His pack. And his future.

He was home and he knew it.

"I'M JUST going to say this straight out. You're rusty, Tucker. Not sharp this preseason. Not anywhere close to your usual level." Banner picked up a piece of paper and studied it for a second.

The large wooden desk not only separated them, but also dominated the entire office. It also provided a distinct professional persona that carried through clearly. This wasn't about socialization. No. This was all business. And that concerned Tucker.

Players had whispered they thought Banner was making up for other shortcomings with that beast of a desk. Right now, Tucker didn't care. He had other problems. Namely, being called in for a one-on-one with the manager. The tone could only be called serious and tension permeated the air.

Tucker tapped his fingers on his thigh. His heart picked up speed as a healthy dose of trepidation washed over him. He felt like an eight-year-old visiting the principal's office.

"You're hitting one-twenty-five and your infield play is sloppy. Too many errors and not enough offensive production." Banner returned the paper to the desk and met Tucker's gaze solidly. "What's going on with you?"

Tucker ran one hand through his hair. "I don't know, sir. It's just not clicking for me yet this year." He swallowed and hastened to add, "But it will. I *know* it will."

In all his years of playing baseball, Tucker had never been in this type of predicament before. Teams fought over him, they pursued him. They never took him to task for his less than stellar play.

Damn it. Raking him over the coals was one thing, but his gut told him that Banner had other ideas. A lump formed in his throat as he considered what Banner's plans might be. Trades happened every day early in the season. Demoting players to the minors also was common, though rare for a player of his reputation and caliber without an injury rehab needed.

Tucker studied Banner carefully, trying to catch a hint of what was to come next. He needed to brace himself and prepare for the worst while hoping for the best. Unfortunately, Banner had his poker face on.

"Nothing happening in your life that is a distraction?" Banner asked.

Tucker shook his head. "No, sir. Everything is on the up and up."

"No fights with your latest girlfriend? No problems at home?"

"No. Gloria and I are fine." Tucker swallowed heavily. "No problems at home either."

The answer rolled off his tongue. Since he'd been an outcast from day one, he didn't consider anywhere home. Except in Preston. With his team. The one place he'd settled down after years of hopping from town to town.

Banner's lips thinned a tiny bit and his eyebrows furrowed.

Tucker lowered his chin to stare at his folded hands on his lap. He caught the flash of inquisitiveness on Banner's face and needed to dissuade his line of thinking and fast.

"Do you miss your pack? Need more time with them?"

Hell, no. "Nope. I'm good." Tucker lifted his chin and met Banner's gaze. By damn he wasn't going to divulge his deepest secret. Not here. Not now. Besides, Banner would probably consider it a ploy for mercy. Tucker never asked for leniency in his life and wasn't about to start now.

Banner sat back and folded his arms across his chest. "Are you burned out? Tired of baseball?"

"No way." Tucker leaned forward, making the old wooden chair creak in the process. "Baseball is all I've ever wanted to do. I love the game." A hint of desperation trickled into his sincere tone.

"What about your teammates? Are you getting along with them?"

Tucker grinned slightly in halfhearted amusement. "Are we including Trigger?"

Banner snorted. "We'll just consider him the exception in this particular discussion."

"Good enough." Tucker sat back. "The guys are great. You saw for yourself today. We're brothers. On and off the field. Even the rookies are fitting in."

"You know, sometimes it does a player good to spend some time in the minors. Get your head on straight. A new environment, new team. That can jump-start a guy's career. Just look at Graham."

Graham, the team's best pitcher, was called up from the minors in the middle of the season last year. He'd rediscovered himself after a rocky patch, and flourished with the Predators. In addition, he'd found his mate in the process.

Well, shit. His fears seemed to be coming true. The last thing he wanted to do was suffer a demotion to the Double-A or Triple-A leagues. However, he couldn't argue the fact that his play sucked thus far this season.

For a long moment, Banner sat quiet.

The wait worked on Tucker's nerves even more. *No matter what, I'm not going to beg or plead.*

16

Just as Tucker bit his lip to keep from asking, Banner opted to speak. "I don't know what's going on with you, but I think you can make it right."

Hope flared. Tucker held his breath.

"There's no doubt you're good for this group. You keep things light and fun with all the guys. Every team needs a couple of players like that."

Banner rested his forearms on the desk and stared at Tucker. "For now, I'm putting Lance as the starter in your place, beginning with the opening day game."

Tucker's mouth fell open. He promptly closed it. Pride forced him to maintain eye contact. *Keep it together, Tucker. Yelling at Banner won't solve a thing.* Neither would growling at him as his inner beast did in his mind.

"Get your head on straight and back in the game. Earn back your starting spot. Prove to me that you still love the game."

Tucker nodded just once, too stunned to think past the fact that he'd just been replaced.

"We're not trading you, although a short trip to the minors isn't out of the question," Banner continued. "Bring up your level of play and show me that I made the right choice."

"Yes, sir." Tucker stood and strode toward the door, working hard to appear in control when his frustration and anger raged inside him.

"Tucker?"

"Yeah?" He paused with his hand on the knob.

"I'm rooting for you, kid. Show me what I know you can do."

With one more look, Tucker opened the door and escaped out into the hallway, still reeling from what had just happened.

He trotted down the hall and out of the building, pausing only long enough to punch a nearby large plastic trash can, sending it flying.

Why me? Why now?

No answers came.

What am I going to do?

Nothing short of figuring out where his skills and mind had gone would do. Unfortunately, no matter how hard he delved into the situation, he still came up empty.

One thing did pop into his mind. He recalled the party thrown by the team's owner scheduled for that evening. The same one Gloria had been pestering him constantly about attending. They had dinner reservations first, though.

Just because his day officially sucked didn't mean he had to cancel everything, go home, and mope like a four-year-old. Even though he really wanted to. Life didn't stop just because his career got a little off track.

Besides, the party would have free liquor. The scales tipped.

After checking his watch, he made a decision. "Party time it is."

His gaze raked the parking area, landing on the jet-black Porsche parked in the front row. His pride and joy, purchased the first year he'd joined the Predators. A sign of his affluence and success. Now, that prestigious lifestyle was in jeopardy.

He'd worked for years to pull himself out of the poverty he'd grown up with. Never did he want to go back to digging through the trash for leftover food or shivering in the winter because there was no money for heat or thick clothing. His mother tried her best, but with no pack and no family support, she was pretty much destined for failure.

I'm not going back there. No way.

He attempted to wave off the worry, but failed. His gut churned as his mind whirled with the decision set down by Banner moments before.

"I can't fix it this very minute. So, might as well shelve it for tonight." Perhaps the evening ahead would give him ample opportunity to forget his problems. At least for one night.

With a hurry in his step, he headed toward his car.

Chapter 3

"CHEERS TO a great fucking day." Tucker tipped the small glass of whiskey and gulped the liquid down. The burn barely registered after drinking so many in the past couple of hours. The buzz, on the other hand, hit him strong and fast, making him smile fleetingly. He set the glass down on the wet bar counter. "Hit me again."

He'd originally decided to snub the team party held at the baseball team owner's house. After all, he wasn't in the right frame of mind for a celebration. Then, things changed and all he wanted was to have a few drinks and forget the past several hours.

Right now, he'd call his plan successful.

The assortment of rich, famous, and popular celebrities in attendance didn't interest him. Not as much as the booze did.

"Hey, buddy."

Tucker glanced up to find Dixon approaching. "Wanna drink?" He waited for the glass to be refilled before lifting it a little wobbly into the air.

"No thanks. Still have one." Dixon held out his beer.

Tucker clanked the drinks together hard. "To…." Liquid sloshed over his hand and down his shirt. "Well, shit." He wiped at the quickly spreading darkness on his white silk shirt.

"Better run that under water before the stain sets in." Dixon took the shot glass from Tucker's hand and placed it back on the bar.

The words took a second to sink in. "Yeah. I guess." He started to stand, had to pause to gain his balance, then shook his head to chase the spinning from his mind. He stared at Dixon in curiosity. "What are you? One of those… butlers?" He had to think for a long moment but finally managed to get the correct word out.

Dixon snort. "I just know a few things. Like you've been sitting here getting wasted."

"Seemed like a good thing to do."

"Care to tell me why?"

Tucker turned to his friend and shrugged. "Banner benched me."

"What?" Dixon leaned closer as if he hadn't heard correctly above the music.

"Banner benched me. A rookie took my starting spot." The admission still stung.

At the time, he'd thought that was the worst thing that could happen. *Yeah, right.* His day only went downhill from there.

"Uh-huh. You *do know* that just because you temporarily lost your starting spot on the team isn't a reason to drink yourself into a stupor, right?" Concern flashed in Dixon's amber eyes.

"It is when my girl walks out because I've been demoted to the backup role behind a mouthy rookie." He'd told Gloria what happened at dinner. She declared him past his prime and on the way down the ladder of success. Not only that, she told him she'd been seeing another guy. *Rightfully so*, she'd told him, as she intended to marry up the line of wealth and Tucker was going in the other direction. She'd stormed out, calling someone else to pick her up.

Tucker paid the bill, hopped into his Porsche, and headed toward the party. The lure of free drink and a potential hookup too much temptation to resist.

"She told me that I wasn't good enough if I wasn't a starter. My value was directly related to my salary, and my stock was dropping fast." Her selfishness cut him to the bone. Still did.

Dixon grimaced at Tucker's explanation and anger heated his eyes. Then he simply studied Tucker for a long moment. "Yeah, that sucks. Big time. Still no reason to kill half your brain cells, though. Especially for a bitch like that."

"That's what you think." Tucker's buzz started to fade with the discussion of his numerous personal problems.

Dixon rested his hand on Tucker's back and nudged him toward the front door. "We'll see if you're still saying that tomorrow morning."

"Where are we going?"

"To my house. You can crash there and sleep it off. Better than staying here or trying to drive." Dixon opened the door, directed Tucker through, and straight to Dixon's car.

"I don't wanna go. I want to drink." Tucker resisted.

"Look, buddy. I'm not leaving you here to your own devices. Either cooperate and I take you to my house, or I'll get reinforcements to help me load you up and drop you off on Banner's doorstep."

Glancing around the room, Tucker made out a couple of Preston players. He knew if Dixon asked, they'd close ranks, hog-tie him, and toss his ass in the back of a truck. No doubt about it.

Better to give in and fight another day. After all, he had enough issues with Banner without showing up out of the blue and drunk. "Okay. Okay."

Tucker shuffled his feet but didn't bother to protest any further. The determination on his friend's face told it all. Either Tucker complied or Dixon would follow through with his threat. In order to maintain his still halfway decent reputation, Tucker obliged Dixon. *For now.*

After sliding into the passenger seat of a decent-sized SUV, Tucker relaxed into the posh leather seats with a small grin. "Nice, bro. Really nice."

Dixon closed the passenger door, then hurried around to climb into the driver's seat. He settled quickly before shoving the key in the ignition. "I'm not much for expensive gadgets and such, but a little luxury now and again is needed." He frowned over at Tucker. "You puke in my car and I'll personally feed you to the sharks in the ocean."

"Not happening. I can hold my liquor." Tucker held his hands up in the air, then belched.

Dixon scowled, but remained mute, then pulled out of the lavish twisting driveway and onto the road.

For a long time, Tucker did nothing more than lightly doze, not up to watching the streetlights fly by. Much better on his stomach to just focus on immobile objects like the moon in the sky. Without a steady infusion of alcohol, his mind had cleared quite a bit while leaving him with a carefree, happy mood.

The best of both worlds and complements of his speedy shifter metabolism.

The car slowed in a quiet cul-de-sac before Dixon pulled into the driveway of a modest two-story house. While not particularly wide, the upper level added economical space and a bit of class to the otherwise ordinary structure. Beige in color, the home sported landscaping around the edges and a medium-sized oak tree standing in the front yard. An immaculate yard spoke of professional care or a homeowner with a green thumb. Tucker didn't know about Dixon's skill with plants and grass, but as much as the team was on the road, surely he hired someone to do the work that kept it looking cared for and pristine.

While most professional players tended to invest in large houses and pricey vehicles, Dixon reminded him of an average man. Nothing too flashy. At least what he'd glimpsed thus far.

Dixon clicked on a device attached to his sun visor, waited for the garage door to rise, then pulled into the garage. Once inside, he turned the vehicle off and hit the button once again.

Darkness surrounded them, but Tucker could see well enough with his enhanced eyesight, thanks to his wild dog genetics.

"Come on. Let's get inside." Dixon stepped out, closing the car door behind him.

Tucker took a second to find the latch, but finally managed to open the door and step out. He shoved it with his butt, hearing the light click when it caught.

Instinctively, he followed Dixon into the house, not stopping until he nearly bumped into his teammate waiting at the bottom of a staircase.

"Bedrooms are upstairs. Let's go."

Tucker glanced up and shook his head. "I'd rather crash down here."

"Not happening." Dixon stepped behind Tucker and gave him a hard nudge. "Climb."

As much as he wanted to argue, Tucker didn't have the gumption or the energy. Besides, he felt too mellow to debate anything. He'd much rather laugh and have a good time instead. The carefree side of his inebriation was thankfully still in effect.

Tucker managed to navigate his way up with the help of the handrails and Dixon's steadying hand on his back. His legs felt oddly weak and a little rubbery. Like he'd run two dozen wind sprints on the practice field. With no real idea of a destination, he simply put one foot in front of the other, deciding he'd figure out the details once he arrived on the second floor.

He hit the upper level and paused.

Dixon strode ahead, grabbed Tucker by the arm and halfway dragged him to a nearby bedroom, not stopping until the back of Tucker's knees bumped into the mattress on the bed.

"Sit before you fall."

Tucker didn't have time to complain before Dixon tugged his shirt upward, lifting Tucker's arms in the process. Coolness wafted across his bare skin, helping to clear his head just a smidgen. Feeling good, he perked up enough to check out the new scenery. A regular bedroom, complete with nightstand, bed, and bathroom. Along with the lighter-haired Dixon who dominated the room with his sheer presence.

Dominated. The term floated through his mind a couple of times, sticking soundly when he raked his teammate with his gaze.

"Hand over those keys too."

"What keys?" Tucker couldn't quite put the pieces together on Dixon's question.

Dixon rolled his eyes, then dug into Tucker's pocket.

A zing flashed up Tucker's spine and landed in his groin. The accidental groping brought his libido back to life. Big time. Along with sending blood rushing to his quickly growing erection.

Dixon's hand fisted and jerked out of Tucker's pants. The flash of metal in the light told Tucker that Dixon found what he sought. "Even though your car isn't here, this should keep you grounded tonight. I don't want you tempted to make your way back to that place and try to pick it up. We'll do that tomorrow when you're nice and sober."

The words flew at Tucker, but all he could think about was the sensation of Dixon digging in his pocket. *The back of his hand rubbing on my aching cock felt so damn good.* He had no idea it would fire up his desires and make him want to growl in demand for Dixon to do it again. Too bad he didn't have to search a bit longer.

Blinking at the unusual thought, he watched Dixon jam the keys into his own pocket, before carrying the shirt into the bathroom straight ahead, turning the water on, and rinsing the garment. The simple act didn't catch his attention nearly as much as the movement of strong legs presently covered by khaki slacks and the wide, muscular shoulders flexing under the casual emerald-green oxford. The short, light brown hair added to the appeal as did the complementary amber color of Dixon's eyes. The whole package. Sexy, primed, and primal. *And right here for the taking.*

He drew in a breath, caught the unique scent of Dixon and felt his cock spring to life.

Insight hit him like a Mack truck. He wanted Dixon. No ifs, ands, or maybes. Just right now. Nothing else would do.

He tilted his head, let his gaze slide down to Dixon's ass, and grinned. "You're damn hot."

Dixon turned to stare at him with a befuddled expression on his face. His eyebrows furrowed as he flipped the shirt under the water with strong, sure hands.

The same hands Tucker wanted roaming his body, clutching his butt, and jerking Tucker down on Dixon's thick cock.

Tucker had never even looked at another man the way he did Dixon. He'd been straight. Until this moment. "Goes to show what I know."

"What?" Dixon squeezed out the shirt, filled the sink with water, turned off the faucet, then lightly dropped the garment back in.

Too turned-on to consider this new development in his sexual preferences, Tucker stood up, undid his pants, and let them drop to his knees. His erection sprang free easily since he rarely wore underwear.

"I'm horny, and you're one fine piece of ass." Reaching down, Tucker began to strum himself.

Dixon's lips parted, but no words emerged.

Tucker smiled as the unmistakable aroma of lust permeated the air. Not just from him, but from the gray fox shifter a few feet away. If that wasn't telltale sign enough, Dixon's slacks sported a decided tent. A large one at that.

His arousal level doubled.

"Fuck me." The request easily rolled off his tongue.

Dixon wiped his hand on a towel hanging in the bathroom before slowly approaching, his eyes never leaving Tucker's face. "You're drunk and don't know what you're doing."

"Oh, I know what I'm doing all right." Tucker licked his lips. "I'm gonna taste your cock." He reached out and fumbled with Dixon's zipper. After Tucker lost his grip twice, Dixon took matters into his own hands and finished the task.

Tucker whimpered as he found Dixon's shaft covered by soft cotton material. Not to be deterred, he leaned forward and lipped the area, smiling when he felt the dick jump under his mouth.

"Big man. Big hands. Big cock." He used his teeth to pull at the material while shoving at the waistband of Dixon's pants. They slid down just in time for Tucker to grab the boxers on the way, leaving Dixon's cock free and ripe for viewing.

He eyed the impressive shaft for a couple of seconds before opening wide and taking the mushroom head into his mouth.

Dixon groaned, the sound carrying lightly through the room. "Tucker...."

"Mmm." He bobbed and took more into his mouth, laving the thick cock with his tongue.

"Tucker. Damn. Wait. Not like this." He clasped onto Tucker's shoulders but didn't push him away.

All Tucker heard was the hesitation in Dixon's voice and a desperate need from deep inside insisted he do something to sway the odds solidly into his favor. For once and for all. The fact that Dixon didn't step away, along with the increasing scent of heightened arousal gave him the tenacity to press the issue.

He reached around, grasped Dixon's butt cheeks, and tugged him closer while adding vacuum to the blowjob he was presently performing. Drawing on what he'd liked in the past, Tucker gave Dixon everything he had, despite his lack of experience on this end. Nothing mattered more than convincing Dixon to climb into the bed and fuck him until the cows came home. He bobbed. He licked. He gave.

"Tucker. Damn." Dixon ran his hand through Tucker's hair. "So good, but you're going to make me come."

For a moment, Tucker debated on how to proceed. As much as he wanted to taste Dixon's cum, he wanted to be taken even more.

Pulling back, he let Dixon's cock exit his mouth before grinning. "You ready to fuck me?"

Hesitation once again clouded Dixon's face.

"I think you are." Tucker stood up as he used one hand to stroke Dixon's shaft. "I want you. Bad." He leaned in, pressed his lips against Dixon's, and caressed them with all the finesse he could gather.

After only a second, Dixon responded. He opened his mouth, licked at the seam of Tucker's lips, then plundered. Deep. Skillful. Intense.

The hottest kiss Tucker had ever experienced happened to be from a man and his own teammate. The realization proved fleeting as Dixon ran his hands over Tucker's chest a couple of times before heading south, shoving Tucker's clothes into a pile around his feet.

Automatically, Tucker stepped out of the puddle of clothes, then gasped as Dixon found his aching cock. White heat shot through his system, adding to the unbridled passion already set free.

"I need you. Now." He uttered the words between kisses.

Dixon licked along Tucker's jawline, then over his shoulder. "Mmm."

Tucker could have stood there all day, enjoying the multiple sensations that Dixon poured on him. Would have if his randy dick didn't begin to throb in high demand. The hand job pushed him higher but not near enough. Nothing short of bending over and letting Dixon take him would do.

"Dixon. Please. Fuck me." He stepped back to read Dixon's expression.

Hot, sultry hunger reflected in Dixon's eyes as well as his features. His jaw tightened as his nostrils flared. Large hands reached out to caress Tucker's nipples into pebbles while Dixon's chest expanded with increasing speed.

The scent of arousal hung in the air. Unmistakable. Delicious. Potent. And all too addictive.

"Are you sure?" Dixon whispered.

"Absolutely." Tucker smiled wickedly. "I want you to be the first to tap my ass." Never had he thought he'd say those words. Yet, nothing else would do. He'd never remotely thought about bending over for anyone. Except Dixon. Something about the man made Tucker want to cry out with unfulfilled need. For the moment, anyway.

Dixon's lips parted as his amber eyes flashed and darkened a hue or two. He sidestepped to a bedside table, opened the top drawer, and pulled out a white tube. After removing the cap, he squeezed a generous dollop onto his palm, and spread it all over his cock.

The action whetted Tucker's desire even more. "How do you want me?"

Dixon tilted his head as if pondering the question. "On your back. I want to watch your face as I fuck you."

Tucker climbed to the center of the bed and spread out.

Dixon followed him, edging between Tucker's spread legs. Instinctively, Tucker bent his knees and splayed his thighs, making his hole an easy target.

Another squirt of gel and Dixon tossed the lube to the side of the bed. He ran his finger down Tucker's crack before dipping the tip of one finger inside.

The chill startled Tucker even as Dixon's touch warmed him right back up.

"I can't wait to taste you." Dixon smiled, bent over, and ran his tongue along the length of Tucker's cock at the same time he pressed his finger inside.

The dual sensations elicited a moan from Tucker and set forth another wave of passion. His hips arched in reaction.

Dixon continued to suck, alternating with flicking his tongue over the sensitive tip and licking. At the same time, he plied Tucker with his fingers. One digit soon became two as he delved deeper and worked the snugness into relaxation.

"This is going to be so damn hot."

Tucker managed a small grin as he rocked his pelvis in a futile attempt to hurry Dixon up. "You're driving me crazy."

Dixon smiled back with excited promise. "And you're sexy. So fucking sexy. I can't wait to shove balls-deep in your ass and feel you come."

"Do it," Tucker challenged, eager to receive more than a couple of fingers in his ass.

"Patience, buddy." Dixon edged forward, removed his touch, then placed the tip of his cock at Tucker's entrance. Since shifters didn't carry disease, there was no need for a condom. "I want this to be perfect."

Tucker held his breath, then moaned when Dixon began peppering kisses along his torso and finally up to his neck.

In return, Tucker ran his hands over Dixon, taking advantage of the opportunity to learn the hills and valleys of Dixon's highly muscular and conditioned chest and arms. Everywhere he could reach, he explored. The feel of Dixon's soft skin along with the ridges added another element to the already potent potion. He opened his mouth, met Dixon's questing lips, and thrust his tongue inside for a quick foray.

Dixon adjusted his position while maintaining the lip-lock, took the weight of his upper body onto his hands, braced on either side of Tucker's head, then nudged forward.

Pressure and resistance captured Tucker's attention. He pressed his heels into the mattress, angled his hips, and felt Dixon's cock enter. A sharp sting accompanied the invasion.

Tucker drew in a breath, closed his eyes, and held on to Dixon's back with a strong grip.

"Nice and easy, Tucker. We're not in any rush."

Tucker opened one eye to peer up at Dixon. "That's what you think." He used his leverage to surge upward, taking more of Dixon's erection inside.

Fullness and a spark of pleasure began to replace the discomfort. Tucker lifted again, opening himself to another gentle thrust by Dixon.

Dixon stopped his momentum and showered Tucker with light caresses with his lips and eager licks over Tucker's chest and shoulders. He nuzzled Tucker's cheek and teased his earlobe. "Okay?"

Tucker growled at the halt in the main action, lifted his head, and nipped at Dixon's biceps. He wanted more. Needed everything. The sweetness he'd appreciate later, but right now he was going up in flames.

Dixon chuckled and stared down at Tucker. "Is that a yes?"

"Yes." Tucker grabbed Dixon's hips and pulled.

Dixon thrust, burying himself completely.

The pain disappeared just as fast as it had appeared, leaving Tucker with nothing but rippling heat and an unbelievable sensation of being filled. Something inside clicked, setting his restraint free in a zealous quest for the pinnacle.

With Dixon covering his body, he could do little more than explore with his hands, nibble, and kiss. He gyrated his lower body as much as possible, but found himself limited with Dixon's presence on top of him.

"Damn, Tucker." Dixon dropped down to settle his weight on top of Tucker, their skin brushing with every breath. With Dixon bracing himself on his forearms, closeness became the precedent.

Tucker soaked it up for a minute, then squirmed in encouragement for Dixon to get busy. "Fuck me." He punctuated the order with a quick nip to Dixon's chin.

Dixon chuckled. "Topping from the bottom. I had no doubt."

Tucker wasn't sure what Dixon meant and his brain didn't have enough blood left to think past his present needs. All he knew was that he needed to be taken and Dixon wasn't moving. Frustrated, he tried to sit up only for Dixon to press him right back down.

"Where are you going?" Dixon's eyebrows furrowed.

Tucker clamped down with his muscles on Dixon's cock, growled, and sharply nibbled on the thick muscle of Dixon's shoulder right in front of him. "If you're not going to fuck me, then roll over and I'll fuck myself on your cock."

Dixon's mouth fell open. His eyes narrowed, then flashed with intense desire. "Do you know what you're asking for?"

Tucker flashed his fangs. "Yeah. Now fuck me already."

Dixon started to move. Fast. Hard. No more tentative motions. Nope. Dixon meant business as he pounded into Tucker, sinking deep on every stroke.

Wanton wildness took over. Tucker yipped. He writhed. He countered every thrust. It wasn't enough. Needing more, he bracketed Dixon's hips with his legs, opening himself up to anything Dixon had to give.

In return, Dixon found a new gear. He stroked powerfully in and out, then edged his body a little higher. The new angle caused him to hit a hot spot with each down stroke.

Immense pleasure shot through Tucker. He cried out, wrapped his arms around Dixon, and arched his back to get closer to the fiery edge. He'd never felt anything this intense and knew the imminent climax would be one for the record books.

Dixon raked his fangs over Tucker's pec. "Come for me."

The slight sting notched Tucker ever closer. The mumbled command didn't hurt either.

Dixon plowed inside, hitting his gland. Once. Twice. A third time.

Tucker growled, then gasped as suddenly he launched into rapture. The tingling started in his groin, but quickly zipped through the rest of his body. One acutely sharp tightening was quickly followed by an explosion. Tucker hit the first crest with a howl of ecstasy. Over and over he peaked, each one punctuated with a cry of some sort, a plea for more and a celebration of sexual bliss. Panting, he locked his gaze with Dixon's, admired the scrunching up of Dixon's face, and the way his lips pulled back in an odd smile. The expression of coming. Hard.

Tight pressure inside snared his focus. He drew in air as Dixon lodged deep inside, his knot buried and swollen, locking them together. Warmth where they were connected entered into the equation, adding to the amazing pleasure, kicking it up another notch. Time flew by, leaving Tucker unable to say how long it lasted, just that he never wanted it to end.

All too soon minor quakes racked Tucker's body, leaving him spent, sated, and damn content.

Dixon's shoulder loomed right in front of Tucker's mouth. He heard the ragged breathing in his ear and felt the hard tremble that went through Dixon. Sweat coated Dixon's skin and the addition of Dixon's weight felt good. Addictive good.

Tucker found himself placing kisses on Dixon's neck, needing to ease his partner down with quiet affection, a shower of appreciation as well as a precursor to what might happen. Later. After they had time to catch their breath.

As if reading his mind, Dixon sat up, peered down at Tucker, and grinned wryly. "That was one hell of a ride."

"Uh-huh." Tucker found himself smiling back. Dixon's knot had started to ease considerably.

Dixon tilted his head and sobered for a moment. "You okay?"

"Splendid." Tucker wanted to wipe away the concern he read on Dixon's face. The sentiment touched him, but there was no reason for it. Not when he felt better than he had in days. He lifted his hand and cupped Dixon's cheek. "I'm perfect."

Relief replaced worry in Dixon's eyes. "Good." He turned his head and kissed Tucker's palm.

The light brushing of lips jolted Tucker back into the realm of sexual need. With something more personal. More emotional.

Except for one thing. "I have to pee."

Dixon chuckled, pulled out, and rolled to the side.

The movement of Dixon's cock in his ass stirred up desire even more.

"Then you should go." Dixon moved to the edge of the bed and stood. "I'll use the spare bathroom. You take this one."

"Deal." Tucker remained still, watching the snap and flex of Dixon's muscles as he walked out of the room.

A warning tingle from his bladder put Tucker into motion. He slid off the bed and made a straight line for the bathroom, his steps sure and stable, testament to the fact that the alcohol had largely worked its way out of his system.

As he washed his hands afterward, he absently checked himself out in the mirror at the same time. "Damn." He had a goofy expression on his face along with a grin. That made sense considering how he felt—happy and outrageously horny.

An oddity. Normally after a robust round of hot sex, he was sated. Occasionally, he'd drag things out longer, if the girl really revved his motor. He couldn't recall feeling this good right afterward, though. As if it was different. More exciting. Better.

Finished with cleaning up, he stepped back into the bedroom and paused at the sight before him. Dixon, in all his naked glory, stretched out on his side across the center of the oversized bed. The gorgeous display of firm muscles, a handsome face, and a large hard-on didn't go unnoticed by Tucker or his suddenly rampant desires.

He licked his lips and simply stared. An urge to flirt blossomed right along with his quickly rising erection. "Well, well. What do we have here?" He crossed his arms over his chest and leaned against the doorjamb.

Dixon grinned and propped his head up with his palm, his elbow braced against the mattress. "Like what you see?"

Oh, yeah. Tucker bit back a smile, preferring to drag out the verbal fun. A version of foreplay. One he enjoyed.

His inner beast barked in excitement, encouraging Tucker to join Dixon on the bed and get busy on the next round. *We'll get there. In a minute or three.* "What big eyes you have."

Dixon blinked. "Eyes? Not cock?" He reached down to take his dick in hand and slowly stroked.

Tucker couldn't hold back the smile. "And what big teeth you have."

"I'm a fox, not the big bad wolf." Dixon smirked. "Or am I?" He rose to hands and knees, then growled low in his throat.

The sound carried through the room and straight to Tucker's aching balls. He answered with a low cry of his own, a promise of submission, if only Dixon would cover him once again.

A bead of moisture emerged from the tip of Dixon's already full cock.

The erotic scene made Tucker's stomach flip, his dick jump, and his inner wild dog pant with exceptional need. His heart sped and his breath caught. In amazement, Tucker realized what he wanted. For Dixon to top him as an alpha forces a submissive to his bidding. He'd gladly roll over and beg, if it earned him Dixon's shaft thrusting into his ass again.

Casually, Tucker walked over to the bed, his eyes never leaving Dixon. "Gonna fuck me again?"

Dixon's eyes turned molten. "Oh, yeah. There's no doubt about it." Sitting back on his haunches, Dixon gestured to the mattress. "Ass in the air this time."

The words sent a tidal wave of heat through Tucker's veins and into his cock, which began to throb in anticipation.

He didn't waste time in climbing onto the mattress, halting near Dixon, then looking back when Dixon didn't immediately move to cover him. "Change your mind?"

"Hell, no." Dixon found the previously discarded tube of gel, squirted some out, and rubbed the lube over Tucker's rear.

The coolness made Tucker draw in a breath before the exquisite sensation of Dixon pressing a couple of fingers into his hole warmed him right back up. He angled back in anticipation of something bigger and harder.

"Enough teasing. Fuck me already." The words gritted out between his teeth.

Dixon lightly slapped him on the right cheek. "Patience. I'll fuck you when I'm ready."

The lippy comment only jacked Tucker up higher. He'd never considered how men screwed, the way of things, the details in the bedroom. Yet, he had not a single complaint. Well, one. Dixon wasn't moving fast enough to get his cock inside Tucker's eager ass.

Staying the course, Dixon didn't do more than prepare Tucker, tormenting him with anticipation in the process.

"Damn, Dixon. Please." A whimper followed.

Tucker never recalled begging before, but he couldn't stop himself. He needed this more than he needed his next meal. His next breath. His next… anything.

Dixon rained kisses down Tucker's spine while he reached around and took Tucker's cock in hand. He stroked lightly, paying extra attention to the mushroom head.

Sparks of pleasure rushed over Tucker. He moaned in response. "Like that?"

"Hell, yeah."

Dixon continued to play with Tucker's shaft for a few moments longer before dipping farther back and cupping the low hanging sac. He rolled the balls gently, then raked his fangs carefully over Tucker's lower back.

The aggressive nature of the near biting shot Tucker's libido through the roof. "Now."

Dixon pressed his erection against Tucker's hole, then shoved.

"Shit." The biting pain stole Tucker's breath. He jerked, then shoved back when the hurt dissipated as quickly as it arrived.

"Okay?" Dixon remained still.

The lack of motion frustrated Tucker. He needed action. Hard thrusting. To be taken like the animal he was. "Yeah. Just…." He grunted, then yipped as Dixon surged in and out with power.

"Yes. Oh, hell, yes." Tucker met him in counterpoint.

The primal coupling tore away what remained of Tucker's inhibitions and let loose his wild side. He lowered to his forearms for a couple of strokes, moaned, then went back up to all fours to shove back and meet Dixon's every thrust. He writhed, wiggled, and rocked with the motions, needing every inch Dixon could give him and more.

His inner beast howled with excitement.

Tucker followed suit as he slammed into climax with the force of a runaway train.

Chapter 4

TUCKER WOKE languidly, finding himself on his side in a large bed, facing the window. Bright sunlight streamed through and onto his face, announcing the day had begun. All well and good, except Tucker was not motivated to rouse. Not when a warm body nestled against his back, the soft skin providing a soothing quality that he wasn't ready to abandon. In addition, the sheet rested across his lower stomach, already tented with his morning wood, a precursor to a beautiful day in bed. If he had his way.

He grinned wickedly to himself. *Obviously all the sex last night hasn't put a dent in my rampant horniness.*

That caught his attention. Big time.

Sex last night.

The thought jarred something in his brain, bringing reality back in a rush.

He froze and frantically searched his memory. The images rushed through his mind in a whirlwind of erotic pictures. The intent to get drunk to forget his problems for a while, Dixon's intervention, the overwhelming horniness and desire for Dixon. The visuals, scents, and sounds. Even the feelings bombarded him with delightful memories. Each stirred up his sexual desire to greater levels. Then the screwing. Oh, yeah. That he couldn't forget.

He hadn't gotten it out of his system last night—he'd only just awakened it.

He clenched his rear, finding a decided soreness that he'd never experienced before. His back door had always been off-limits. His other lovers didn't seem to mind. The ladies wanted his cock buried in their greedy holes instead of delving into some kinky reversal of roles.

But he'd never been with a man before. *Until last night.* When Dixon climbed on board and took them both on a trip to an amazing ecstasy. The level of rapture he couldn't remember experiencing nor had he thought possible.

Something clicked between him and Dixon. Clicked so well that he was more than primed for another round or three.

Except one tiny fact didn't make the least bit of sense—he was straight. Never looked twice at another man other than as a friend, acquaintance, or a teammate. Certainly not a potential lover.

Now, he rested in another man's arms as naked as the day he was born. Comfortably. Happily. Lazily.

Hell, he'd never cuddled with the women he'd slept with. Didn't want to. Today, he found sliding out of bed and away from his male lover more than difficult.

Holy shit. I rolled over and let Dixon fuck me like a bitch in heat. Let, hell. I begged for it.

The outrageous thought spurred him into action. He slid off the side of the bed, scoured the room, found his clothes, and quickly slid them on. Only when he buttoned up his pants did he spare a glance to the bed.

The sight stole his breath.

Dixon stared at him, with his head propped up with his elbow, his short light brown hair tousled from sleep. If that wasn't sexy enough, his muscular shoulders, chest, and abs were on display, framed and contrasted by the white linens against his tanned skin. The tip of his cock peeked out from under the rumpled sheet, full and ready for action. The expression on Dixon's face could only be called hungry. Tucker's wayward dick hardened to granite.

Damn.

He immediately felt the loss of body heat and something more. Something he didn't bother trying to name at this moment in time. His head was too busy trying to wrap itself around the obvious evidence of what he'd done.

Reality sank in with sharp clarity. "What did I do?"

Dixon's face clouded. "You don't remember?"

If only it were that simple. For a second Tucker grappled with the impulse to pretend amnesia, to forget what happened and walk away for good. His inner wild dog growled angrily at the thought.

Lying wasn't his thing and now would be a lousy time to start. As tempting and convenient as it might happen to be.

Pulling on his last ounce of decency, he faced Dixon with serious resolve. "I remember everything. Yeah, I was drunk, well, partway, but it's all there. Every moment." With the words came flashes of the erotic bliss from the night before. Stoically, he ignored them along with his aching cock.

This happened every time he broke up with a girl. Got drunk. Slept around. Woke up in an unfamiliar bed. Though never with a man before. A teammate at that.

"So... what's the problem?" Dixon sat up. The action allowed the sheet to dip lower, showing off Dixon's impressive hard-on.

Unable to take his eyes off the other man's shaft, Tucker drew in a deep breath and forced his lust-filled and confused mind back to work. "I'm not gay." The statement sounded weak to his own ears.

Dixon rubbed his five o'clock shadow, drawing attention to his scruffy face, which only added to his overall rugged and handsome appearance.

Stop it, already. Enough ogling.

His self-chastising only made his inner beast bark in disagreement.

"You don't have to be gay, Tucker. Considering you've been dating women, I wouldn't remotely consider labeling you as gay."

Tucker gave a brief nod, still reeling from the stark realization. "You're bisexual."

He jerked his head up. "What? Oh, no. No. I'm straight. Always have been. Just drank too much and...." He swept his arm in a half circle in front of him.

"And we fucked," Dixon finished for him.

"Yeah." Tucker ran his hand through his hair and slipped his shirt back on. The still-damp material clung to his chest, adding a bit of a chill. "It just happened. That's it. Nothing more, nothing less." He caught the momentary flinch in Dixon's face. Guilt landed hard on his shoulders.

Dixon moved to the edge of the bed, then stood.

Tucker purposely diverted his gaze away from Dixon's prominent dick.

"I know you liked it. The way you howled under me when you came. There was no question." Dixon crossed his arms over his chest and pinned Tucker with his gaze.

"I... I...." Tucker shut his mouth. The urge to flee hit him hard enough that he spun and left the room. Long strides carried him down the steps and right up to the front door.

"Damn it, Tucker. Stop running." Dixon called out as he pounded down the stairs, right on Tucker's heels. "We need to talk about this." He jumped ahead, blocking the exit, and forcing Tucker to halt. "You can't walk back to the mansion for your car. Too far. Besides, I still have your keys."

Tucker grimaced at the reminder of what started the whole erotic shenanigans. Dixon digging the keys out of his pants pocket. The resulting caress set his desires free and his whole body on fire with lust.

He forced the thought from his head and focused on the present dilemma. Dixon was right. He had no transportation and his vehicle was miles away. Calling a cab would work, but that would still take time.

"Was what we did so awful?" The thick emotion in Dixon's voice pulled him from his chaotic thoughts.

Tucker lifted his head and looked at his friend, ignoring the magnificent body on display, and studied Dixon's face. Worry coated his expression as well as a hefty dose of self-reproach.

"No." The word tumbled out on a whisper.

He'd been a willing participant all along. Truth be told, he'd instigated the whole event. Thus any regrets and guilt rested solely on his shoulders.

Dixon said nothing for a long moment. "Let me throw some clothes on, and then I'll take you back to your car." He turned and trotted back up the staircase.

Tucker watched him go with a sense of sadness and lingering desire. The flexing and snapping of Dixon's primed muscles as well as his perfectly rounded ass didn't help in the least.

Just jot it down as a wild adventure. Nothing more, nothing less. The sentiment sounded strong but lacked substance, even in his own mind. He blew out a long breath and tried to stop the pounding of his heart. *I slept with Dixon. Get over it already.*

He'd just forget it ever happened. Sew his lips closed on the subject and hope Dixon did the same.

Unfortunately, that scenario didn't have a stellar chance of happening, not the way he'd been falling into pit holes lately.

No sooner had Dixon pulled the SUV out of the driveway than he put them right back on the awkward topic Tucker so wanted to avoid.

"I know you're confused about everything."

"Hell, yes, I'm confused. A week ago I was happily dating Gloria and screwing her any chance I had. Now…." He trailed off, unable to formulate words.

"In case you were wondering, I happened to like what we did. We meshed well. Had a great time. One of the best that I can remember." Dixon spared him a quick glance before focusing on the road once more. "I don't have a single regret and am up to doing it again."

The offer jolted Tucker. He hadn't dealt with the first time, let alone considered there'd be more. Feeling trapped, he lashed out in an effort to finalize things for once and for all. "Look. Like I said before. It just happened. I got drunk. Did something stupid. Like always."

Dixon frowned. "You call that stupid?" His tone carried a sharp edge.

Tucker sighed and ran his hand through his hair. "It was a mistake."

"So you keep saying." Dixon shook his head slightly, still watching the road ahead of him. "I don't agree."

"It's a dumb pattern. When someone breaks up with me, I hit up a club, drink a few, then I find a hot hookup for the night. It's just a tension release. Not undying love." Tucker couldn't help but get a bit defensive. He didn't like himself much at the moment, and Dixon's point on the topic made him feel all that much lower. *And rattled. Definitely rattled.*

"Let me get this straight. You broke up with your girlfriend, couldn't find another woman at the wet bar, saw your opportunity when I took you home, and thought 'what the hell, he's a warm body to fuck'?"

Tucker flinched at the subtle bite in Dixon's voice. He knew he'd hurt his friend's feelings, but didn't know how to be honest without doing so. He wasn't the man Dixon thought he was. Not gay. Not bi. Just a guy that screwed up royally.

A royal screwup that felt so damn right.

He ignored the little voice in his head, unable to deal with the already overwhelming burden.

Being an ass it is.

He drew in air to bolster his rapidly waning intentions. "Yeah. I'd have gone with a woman, but barring that, anyone would do. Even another man."

The tightening of Dixon's face told the story along with a flash of pain in his eyes. Tucker's words hit home. And not in a good way.

Determined, Tucker stayed the course, knowing the only way to get Dixon to lay off was to make him see the impossibility of sex happening again and the fleeting moment that had long since extinguished itself. *Whether it's true or not.*

"I'm sorry if you thought there was more there. It was just another ridiculous drunken caper. We both got our rocks off. End of story."

A tic in Dixon's jaw drew Tucker's attention.

He steeled himself for what was to come.

Nothing did. Not even when they pulled into the parking area outside the mansion. Dixon tossed him the keys. Tucker caught them, opened the door, stepped out of the car, and paused only long enough to mutter a quick "thanks" before making a beeline to his own vehicle. Just as he pushed the fob to unlock the door, an engine revved, and then Dixon drove off in a hurry.

As he turned, the deep blue SUV zipped out of the driveway and back onto the street in quick fashion.

Tucker's shoulders sank, as did his confidence. Not only had he made one hell of a hash out of his life, he'd also led Dixon on and then rejected him point-blank.

Some friend I am.

With that morose thought, he climbed into his car, fastened his belt, and started for home.

Two hours later, Tucker flopped down on his couch and stared at the ceiling of his apartment. He'd gone for a jog, then took a long shower. Still, his mind wouldn't stop replaying the previous night. Images. Sounds. The novel feeling of having a cock shoved up his ass. Just the thought caused his pulse to pick up speed and his libido to sit up and take notice.

Well, shit. Just what I need. Not.

He blew out a breath and tried to piece the puzzle together.

What the hell happened?

He'd intended to get drunk, only managed to get tipsy and feeling good when Dixon dragged him away from the party. Then, he'd gotten up close and personal with the gray fox shifter, the aroma of lust emitting from them both. The next thing he knew was that he had to have the guy. Needed to be topped and fucked like nothing else.

And that's what confused him the most.

He'd never looked at men in that way. *Never.* Even the mated gay couples on the team, he found their banter and mutual affection to be cute, but it never stirred his interest. Then, one evening with Dixon changed the world.

How does a guy become gay after being straight his whole life? What changes to make that switch? How do I turn it back?

Dixon's words came back to him. *You're bisexual.*

Technically, he couldn't argue with the term. He had sex with a man. *Great.* So, why now? Why Dixon? It would be a hell of a lot easier if it had been some stranger. He could chalk it up to a kinky one-night stand and go on with life. Not a possibility when Dixon was a huge part of his daily life during baseball season. They were friends, to boot.

The last thing he wanted was to crush Dixon's feelings, but he didn't dare lead the man on either. Nothing could come of this. Nothing. So, pursuing it was senseless, as he had no intention of repeating the event.

Speaking of, how am I going to face him again? What can I really say?

Deep down, he knew Dixon had hesitated at first in their coupling. Tucker had seduced him with erotic pleasure to get him to jump in with both feet. The responsibility rested heavily on Tucker's shoulders. Except he didn't regret being with Dixon. He just didn't understand how he could come to a point around women but a man never brought about even a hint of desire. Guys were teammates. Friends. Nothing more.

As much as he wanted to blame the event on the liquor he'd consumed, he couldn't. Dishonesty with himself never worked and didn't change a single thing. Besides, he had his own built-in lie detector in the form of his inner animal. The guy called him on it every time.

He'd been well aware of what he wanted to do, encouraged to happen, and then did in Dixon's bed. Maybe the booze loosened him up. Probably did. Still, he was a consenting adult who'd pretty much begged Dixon to take him.

Pretty much? Shit, I begged him, pleaded with him, and did everything in my power to get him to fuck me.

He groaned to himself in embarrassment and disbelief.

Even worse. He had to face Dixon tomorrow morning at practice. If that wasn't bad enough, he prayed the rest of the team hadn't read anything into the fact that Dixon took him home from the party. He could deal with Dixon. Maybe. But, having the whole team pestering him with questions would be the straw the broke the camel's back.

"Maybe getting traded would be a blessing right now."

As soon as he said the words, his inner beast protested with a throaty growl. His conscience agreed.

He'd worked hard to get where he was. On a winning team, surrounded by good people. His salary allowed him luxuries, and he'd settled into a life filled with expensive acquisitions, plenty of women if he wanted them, and a steadiness that he'd craved all his life. Growing up poor and seemingly always on the move taught him many things. Namely, how lucky he'd been to find entry into the professional league.

No guarantees existed in the game, nor in life. Thus, he could find his bubble burst and himself plummeting back down at any point. Real and a definite possibility. If he didn't get his act together.

"But how am I going to get back on my game when I'm still trying to figure out how I became gay and what I'm going to do about it?"

His mind remained void of answers.

"And I'm back to where I started. How am I going to face Dixon again?" He cringed at the inevitable.

He'd shut Dixon down and run like a pack of hounds were on his heels. That worked at the time, but didn't bode well for when they were stuck in the same locker room or hanging out on the same bench.

To get lippy or to be abrupt if Dixon pursued the conversation they'd left open would bring attention from the other guys.

Which meant he'd have to pretend like nothing had happened and pray Dixon didn't corner him with a battery of questions. Hopefully Dixon had listened when Tucker told him that it was just a screwup. *That's right. One hell of a screwup. I'm not into men. Period.* While the words sounded a bit weak to him, he knew Dixon would question them immediately. Something he couldn't allow to happen.

Too many ifs for comfort. What he really needed was a lot of luck.

Too bad his had all turned bad lately.

"DAMN IT to hell." Dixon stormed back inside his house and tossed his keys onto the kitchen table. Anger ruled with worry while hurt pushed for a really close second. He paced across the living room, long strides covering the ground quickly. He cursed the limited space, the lack of an outlet, and the mule-headed Tucker for running. To hear Tucker tell the story, it was all a night of drunken shenanigans, that he regretted today. Dixon believed the opposite. He'd found everything he'd searched for with Tucker. In bed and out.

How long had he watched Tucker from afar? Months? Ever since Tucker joined the team about three years back. Something about him snared Dixon's attention and maintained it. His easy smile, the terrific build, the flash of mischief in his dark eyes. Even the halfway-tamed black wavy locks that Tucker grew out one year only added to his appeal.

Dixon admired from afar, enjoyed their friendship, and wished for something more, knowing it wouldn't likely happen. He'd seen Tucker bounce from woman to woman. Never to a man.

Since Dixon was exclusive with men, that threw a huge monkey wrench into his hopes.

Just when he'd been ready to give up, Tucker, on a rebound from another short-lived relationship, fell into his bed. They'd fit together perfectly, an extension of their easygoing friendship. Everything looked to be on the up and up until Tucker shrugged off their time together like a quick trip to the toilet before hurrying off as if the mouth of Hell had opened and block by block the city was falling in.

The facts added up fast in Dixon's mind. Too bad he'd never get to live up to the rosy dream of being with Tucker as a teammate, friend, and lover. The first two, formerly a given, were now in question as well.

He blew out a deep breath, plopped down on the couch, and rested his head in his hands. "Why, Tucker? Why can't you see what I see?"

He'd caught the profound shock on Tucker's face. Read it in his tense body language and the abrupt escape tactic Tucker employed. He couldn't accept the fact that he'd been with a man, no matter who the guy happened to be. Obviously, in Tucker's own eyes, he was straight. Period. Anything else was cause for alarm.

So, how am I to deal with that? Fight it? Fix it? Or just forget it?

A quitter, he wasn't. Besides, this was far too important to just throw in the towel.

He sat back, letting his head rest on the back of the couch, closed his eyes, and simply thought. Blankness met him.

"How do I make him see we've got something special? Or could have. If he'd get his head out of his ass for a minute."

Silence answered.

The chirping of his phone drew his attention. He dug it out of his pocket, checked the caller ID, and groaned. Against his better judgment, he answered. "Hey, Dad."

"Dixon. Caught the last few games."

Dixon sat forward and prepared himself for another lecture. His father lived and breathed baseball. A hall of famer, Terrance Foxx had all the hitting records during the time he played professionally. Some of those marks remained to this day.

While his father might have been one of the best to ever play the game, he fell short in the fatherhood department, in Dixon's opinion. All they seemed to talk about was baseball, more times than most, including how he could do better. He didn't need to read the appraisals or look up his own stats. His own father never let him forget the numbers or failed to point out ways to do something a tiny bit better. All Dixon wanted was his father's love, not his commentary and criticism.

He'd grown up as a prodigy. Anyone and everyone knew he'd hit the pros. His father pushed for more than that. He wanted Dixon to follow in his footsteps. To be the best of the best. But there was one big difference. Terrance lived for the game. Dixon, not so much.

In contrast, his mother seemed to care less for the game. Sure, she supported them both in the sport, but she didn't live and breathe baseball. She tried to make up for the voids by showering Dixon with attention, encouraging him in his other endeavors. While he appreciated it, he couldn't help but long for his father's approval all the more. He loved her and everything she did for him. Still, she couldn't give him what he ultimately needed—his father's praise.

"You're dropping that outside shoulder just a little right before you swing. If you could keep it up, it would give you more power and less pop-ups."

Dixon bit his tongue and wondered again why he even bothered to answer. It was always the same.

This time, he'd hoped might be different. He could use some sage advice from his old man about matters other than the game. Too bad it didn't seem to be in the works. Not now and probably never.

"Okay." He forced the word out. All he wanted to do was to get out. Run. Exercise. Try to get rid of the pent-up frustration, a complement to Tucker's fast departure and his turning a blind eye to the situation. Sitting on the couch and listening to yet another lecture from his father only made things worse.

I have bigger problems than a minuscule stance correction while hitting.

"Listen, Dad. I need to get going. Have to hit the gym today."

"Good. It always pays to stay in shape. Strengthening workouts will only help your batting average."

I don't fucking care right now. "Yeah. I'll catch you later." He hung up the call before his father could respond. Rude? Probably. But his sanity was worth any irritation on his father's behalf.

Speaking of sanity…. He needed to get out of the house and do something. Sitting around trying to figure out the complex puzzle named Tucker would only drive him insane. The gym provided a much-needed outlet. He could work out and think at the same time.

Perhaps divine intervention might strike while he was there.

Keep dreaming, Dixon. Keep dreaming.

Trotting up the stairs, he quickly changed clothes, ignoring the rumpled bed and the intoxicating scent of Tucker and robust sex still lingering in his bedroom. Since he had no clue how to repeat the fuck session any time soon, he preferred to simply get out of the house and away from the exquisite memories. For now.

He wasted no time in grabbing his keys and heading toward his car.

Chapter 5

No time like the present.

Tucker took a deep breath, then pushed through the doors of the team's locker room.

"Hey, Tucker." Mack gave a small grin as he pulled up his socks. "About time you showed up."

Glancing around, Tucker didn't see Dixon anywhere in sight. Nor did he smell him. Considering all the other aromas found in the locker room, some quite strong, he couldn't really bank on Dixon being absent.

"Hi, Mack." The leopard shifter typically played left field, but could be found at any of the outfielder positions as the need arose. Quiet but friendly, he was a good guy to have around. With a quick wave, Mack made his way outside.

Tucker carried his duffel bag to his locker and set it down on the small bench running nearly the length of the room. He opened the metal door, pulled out his practice jersey, and started stripping down.

"Tucker. Saw you at the party. Man, you were hitting the booze hard." Shorty, the relief catcher, plopped down next to his bag. "Looked like you were trying to bury some problems."

A low growl escaped Tucker's throat. He liked Shorty well enough but drew the line at him digging into his personal life.

Shorty held up his hands. "Right. None of my business." He stood and hastened out the door leading into the dugout.

Tucker took the opportunity to enjoy the silence and familiarity of the Predators team room. Home away from home, in his opinion. At least for most of the year and when they weren't traveling to or from away games.

He grabbed his bag, filled with clothes for a weeklong series, and stuffed it into the locker. They had an abbreviated practice today before leaving on a road trip. Normally, he looked forward to traveling, seeing the other stadiums and the land in between. Today was the exception. He'd rather stay home and avoid the whole ordeal.

No matter how hard he tried, he couldn't get Dixon off his mind. Every waking hour, he found himself returning to the big event, reliving that experience through graphic and hot memories. Along with that came guilt for being such an ass to Dixon and concern about how his friend coped with such a harsh rejection.

"I'm such an idiot."

"Depends on how you look at it."

Dixon's voice startled Tucker. He spun around to see Dixon just inside the doorway, with the strap of his own bag resting on his shoulder. Dressed in loose khakis and a light beige shirt, Dixon looked good. Really good. His light brown hair contrasted with his amber eyes, adding intelligence and character to his handsome face. From the slightly square jaw to the high cheekbones to the small misalignment of his nose, Dixon radiated sexiness. The rest of his body didn't do too badly either. As he stepped closer, the pants tightened over thick muscles, hinting at the power and prime conditioning Dixon carried.

Damn Dixon and his stealth.

How many times had he rehearsed what he'd say when he came face-to-face with Dixon? Dozens? Yet, now that the situation was here, he found himself mute.

"Cat got your tongue?" Dixon stopped a few feet from Tucker and arched an eyebrow. More of a challenge rather than mocking.

"Dixon." Tucker acknowledged him before tugging his shirt off and quickly replacing it with his uniform top. He focused on the task while trying to get his speeding heart back under control along with his raging desire at seeing Dixon again. The last thing he needed was to sport a hard-on in the locker room.

He'd thought the sex appeal would fade quickly. He was wrong.

Dixon's presence alone revved his motor and stoked his libido. The knowledge that Dixon still had to change only added fuel to the already blazing fire.

I'm not gay.

Then why are you panting with want?

48

A great time for my inner wild dog to get chatty. Not. Tucker sighed to himself and countered. *One and done. It's over.*

Keep telling yourself that. I know better.

Dixon moved a couple of steps closer, setting his bag on the opposite bench. His gaze, though, never left Tucker. Tucker knew because he couldn't pry his eyes off Dixon for anything.

If there was another place to get dressed, Tucker would have gladly collected his gear and marched over there. Unfortunately, this was it. With practice starting soon, he really didn't have a choice but to change right in front of Dixon.

He's seen it all anyway. Seen it. Tasted it. Touched it. Fucked it.

The blunt words prodded him to get in gear. After placing his back to Dixon, he shucked his pants, let them fall into a puddle at his feet, then stepped out of the cloth shackles.

"Nice."

Tucker glimpsed Dixon pulling his lips back into an odd grin. He read the body language easily. Dixon was checking the air for pheromones. He'd find them too. Especially since Tucker grappled with his own horniness at the moment.

That or he smells himself on me.

The thought made Tucker bite back a groan. A combination of lust, frustration, and heated anger. "Damn it. I'm not gay."

He had no idea he'd uttered those words aloud until Dixon answered.

"We've been through this. You're bi, Tucker. And that's nothing to be ashamed of." Dixon edged closer. "Think of it this way. You're an equal opportunity lover." He offered up a lopsided smile that could only be called cute.

Tucker quickly scanned the room, finding it empty except him and Dixon. *Thank God.* The last thing he needed was the rest of the team to pick up on what happened between him and Dixon. He'd never hear the end of it.

Pulling up his pants, Tucker fastened the fly and cinched the belt with practiced ease. His socks and shoes followed.

"Tucker?"

Resisting the urge to respond, Tucker fixated on digging out his glove and cap from the locker.

"Tucker. Damn it. Talk to me." Dixon's voice carried exasperation and command.

Ready to go, Tucker turned to face Dixon once more. "Sorry. I'm late for practice."

Before Dixon could say anything, Tucker hurried out the door and into the dugout. A fresh breeze blew across his face, easing the tension a hair.

I can't avoid him forever.

He didn't need to. Just long enough to figure out what the hell went wrong and how to get back on track with the ladies. Or until Dixon got the right message. Whichever came first.

With the promising thought, he jogged onto the diamond.

A small gathering met him.

"Hey, Tucker. Don't worry. You'll regain that starting spot in no time." Ram clapped him on the shoulder.

"Yep. We'll help. Whatever it takes to get you back on track, sign us up," Graham added.

"Always up for more practice. You know that," Mack said.

"I'll help too," Dixon retorted as he approached the group.

Tucker flicked his glance to Dixon briefly before returning to the others. *Of course, they would know by now.* Tucker stared at them all, his shame growing by the second. He did appreciate their support, though.

"Thanks, guys. I just need to work harder and get my head on straight."

"Yeah, you do." Trigger slapped the end of his bat against his cleats, knocking out a few small chunks of dirt. "And fast."

The fact Trigger said something at all impressed Tucker. Normally, the taciturn grizzly shifter had nothing but blunt criticism. For him, this was encouragement. He soaked up the moment. Which could easily be one of the last with the Predators.

His shoulders sagged with the depressing thought.

"Hey, it's a slump. That's it. Nothing more. We all have them." Wiley patted Tucker on the upper arm. "Been there, done that myself. Lived to tell the story too."

Tucker shot him an appreciative but less than happy smile. "I sure hope you're right. The last thing I want to do is leave this team."

"Then let's get to work, buddy." Ram led the way out onto the field.

Tucker swiveled to find Dixon watching him. He studied the gray fox shifter for a few seconds, gave a slow nod of his head in appreciation, then trotted out to his usual place on the diamond. Tucker might have been a jackass when they were alone, but he had more class than to snub Dixon in front of the guys, especially when he made his position clear. They were still friends, or so he thought. However, just because Dixon had his back didn't mean Tucker wanted to chance getting too close. Been there, done that, and had the headache from trying to figure out what in the hell happened, to boot.

He had to set priorities. *Earn my spot back first. The other stuff can wait. Maybe forever.*

He kicked at the dirt around second base, then turned his attention to the plate. Infield practice was about to start, and he intended to do significantly better than yesterday.

Half an hour later, Banner pointed him to the bench while the other players rotated through different positions on the field. Tucker didn't mind the break. Even with the comfortable temperatures, he needed a bottle of cold water to quench his thirst. After digging through the cooler, he found one, then sat down at one end of the bench.

Ram plopped down beside him, craning his head this way and that as if trying to see around the walls of the dugout.

The unusual behavior piqued Tucker's curiosity. "What are you doing?"

"Watching for Wiley's grandmother. She showed up to watch practice today." Ram took a long drink from his water, then stood up, cussed, and immediately sat back down. "Yep. She's headed this way."

"And that's bad why?" Tucker couldn't imagine why a little old lady would have Ram so antsy.

"Because every time she gets within arm's reach, she has to pinch my ass. Makes me feel like a side of beef."

Tucker chuckled. "Rump roast, huh?"

Ram flipped him off.

Sure enough a silver-haired lady trotted down the steps and into the dugout. Her hot pink shorts, top, and matching sandals blinded Tucker for a moment. When he could see again, he couldn't quite get his gaze above her ample bosom. *Holy shit. This is Wiley's grandmother?*

"Oh, there you are, Ram." She smiled wide, ambled over, and patted him on the head. "Stand up so I can get a good look at you."

Ram rolled his eyes but did as ordered.

Tucker bit back a giggle as the lady stared at him like a woman deprived of dessert seeing one of those chocolate Easter bunnies in the store.

"Yep. Still as nicely put together as always. That's good. Can't have you getting all lumpy if you're going to keep up with my grandson."

"Yes, ma'am." Ram sat back down.

Her attention turned to Tucker. "Who do we have here?"

"Tucker. Tucker Wilde." He held out his hand to her.

"Elaine." She took it, tugged him hard into a standing position, then made a circle around him. "Nice. Very nice."

Too stunned by Elaine's strength, it took a second for Tucker to realize what she was doing.

Tucker felt the less than gentle pinch on his posterior and immediately sidestepped. "Whoa."

She grinned wickedly up at him. "You'll do."

Her meaning sunk in. And promptly scared the crap out of him too. Tucker held up his hand. "No, ma'am. You see. I'm not available." He kicked his pokey mind into gear coming up with excuses. *Come on. Before she drags me back into the locker room and commences a dental exam… with her tongue.*

"What's the matter? You don't like mature ladies?"

Well, now that you mention it…. He bit his lip and frantically debated how to answer. *Saggy boobs aren't my thing. Great in theory, but hers stand high and proud, just like a flag on a windy day. They probably jiggle just as much too.*

Argh! Come on. Give me something. Anything.

He struggled through being clueless for a few seconds, then blurted out the first thing that popped into his head. "I'm gay."

All the nearby players snapped their heads around to stare at him in open shock. Ram blinked, then smirked. "Since when?"

"Since… ummm…."

"Oh, hell, no. You're not gay. Not with that nearly endless line of women coming and going from your hotel room on road trips," Shorty said.

Tucker cut a glare at Shorty. He shut up fast.

Elaine stared at Tucker intently, like she was sizing him up for a pair of handcuffs and some funky leather outfit.

He swallowed. "I'm reformed. Yep. Just a couple of days now, but I'm definitely gay."

Ram snickered but covered it with a cough.

"That's too bad, dear." Elaine turned around and eyed the other men in the dugout.

A mass exodus followed.

"Well, shoot." She marched up the stairs and strode along the wall behind home plate.

Ram blew out a long sigh of relief. "She's zany but quite entertaining."

"I'll take your word for it." Tucker felt a little violated by the old lady fondling his rear.

"So, what's this about you turning gay?"

Tucker groaned. "I'm not gay."

"No shit, Sherlock. But, that subtle scent you're carrying of Dixon begs the question of bi." Ram twisted in order to study Tucker.

Well, hell. "I'm straight." The words came out weak even to him.

"Uh-huh. Been there, buddy. I played with the ladies too. Until Wiley."

Belatedly, Tucker recalled that Ram's gate had swung both directions until he mated. "But you knew you were bi."

"Yeah."

For a long time, Tucker said nothing else. He had a dozen questions but couldn't bring himself to ask a single one. Not the right time or the right place. Besides, Wiley's grandmother had cornered Banner. The scene deserved his undivided attention.

The two spoke in low tones, until Elaine reached out and cupped Banner's bottom. He scowled and promptly removed her hand from his body.

"Guess he's off her list too."

Tucker almost felt sorry for the obviously horny lady. But not enough to volunteer himself to make her day. "Poor Elaine."

Ram snorted. "Nothing poor about her. She'll find a guy soon enough. You should see her at the pack parties. Popular doesn't begin to describe it."

Wiley hurried over. "Tell me again why you gifted her with a VIP field pass."

Ram grinned wide. "Because she wanted to watch her favorite grandson play ball and meet his friends."

"Uh-huh. You're trying to drive me to drinking, aren't you, mate?"

"Drinking? No. I have other ideas for stress release." Ram waggled his eyebrows.

Wiley rolled his eyes. "How did I know you were horny?"

"I don't know. How?" Ram fed the question right back at him.

Wiley shook his head and trotted over to corral his grandmother.

Tucker watched the interaction with interest.

Ram turned back to him, still smiling. "You don't know what you're missing."

"With Wiley's grandmother or being mated?" He arched an eyebrow.

Ram laughed. "Your pick."

Like I don't have enough complications in my life already.

Maybe it's high time I find a pretty lady and get laid.

The thought held merit. Bunches of it. He latched onto the idea and vowed to pursue the plan as soon as they arrived at their hotel later today.

DIXON SHUT his hotel door and ambled down the hall. Thankfully, dinner awaited in the cafeteria downstairs. His stomach had been growling almost since the moment they arrived in Florida. The complimentary orange juice didn't do much for him besides prompt his belly to remind his mind that the light lunch had long since worn off.

A giggle and the click of a door caught his attention. He turned toward the sound, found a woman in a snug, very short dress step out of a door, her high heels in hand. Her mussed hair told the story as did the male arm that reached out far enough to pat her rear. She squealed and waved her finger at him. "Such a bad boy. Just the kind that I like."

"Uh-huh."

"I can stay and wait for you...."

"No. I've got team stuff to do. Like I told you before, I'm not looking for more than just a good time."

Dixon froze. He recognized that voice. *Tucker.* There was no doubt about it. Especially when Tucker stepped over the threshold enough for Dixon to easily make out his features. With nothing more than a pair of boxers on, Tucker made quite a lickable vision. Except for one thing—he'd obviously just bedded the girl.

Anger and regret flashed through Dixon. His inner fox snapped in agreement.

We've been here all of two hours and he's already found a woman and gotten laid.

He hated the fact that Tucker had snagged one of the groupies and invited her to his bed. Normally, the guys waited until after dinner to seek out personal entertainment for the night. Tucker, bucking tradition, started early. Whether to reaffirm his straightness in his mind or to show Dixon which side of the fence he firmly stood on, Dixon couldn't say. He just knew that seeing this spectacle hurt.

As he watched, the woman dug out a piece of paper from her tiny purse slung over her shoulder, and handed it to him. "Call me." She smiled, turned, and sashayed down the hall, swinging her hips in open invitation to any male around. Or so it seemed to Dixon who disliked the lady on sight.

I'm such a petty idiot.

He blew out a breath and forced his feet to start moving again. As much as he wanted to storm the room and declare Tucker his and only his, he knew that would be like adding dynamite to an already raging inferno. The resulting explosion would certainly be dangerous and counterproductive.

What did I expect? Undying love from Tucker?

The well-deserved chastisement brought reality into clear focus. He'd enjoyed one magical night. Since then, Tucker avoided him like the plague and obviously found someone else to warm his bed and

provide tension relief. At least this one was a quickie and seemingly a onetime thing if he overheard correctly. That cooled his irritation only marginally.

Frustrated with himself, Tucker, and pretty much the whole world, Dixon punched the elevator button extra hard. He'd rather hit something else, but the decided lack of something or someone nixed that impulse. For now.

Unable to wipe the scene from his mind, Dixon took the elevator down to the ground floor and followed his nose to the cafeteria. He found Trigger and Graham occupying one table in the corner. The way they stared at one another, as if each one completed the other, made him even more jealous and upset with Tucker. *I want what they have. With Tucker.* The fact that it appeared highly unlikely soured his mood.

After finding an empty table across the room from his teammates, Dixon sat down. A waitress immediately brought over a glass of water and a menu. He looked it over quickly and ordered. She hurried off, leaving him happily alone.

"What's tasty today?" Mack pulled out the seat opposite Dixon and plopped down.

Dixon bit back a frown. While he truly liked the other players, that didn't mean he wanted their company right now. Drawing in a breath, Dixon aimed for civil. "I'm not sure, just went with what sounded good."

Mack's eyebrows shot up.

Well, shit. Obviously his tone didn't match his words.

"You sound a bit edgy. Does it have anything to do with why you sat in the front seat on the bus and only spoke with Banner the whole way?"

Dixon had hoped no one paid him much attention. Obviously, Mack, the left fielder noticed. Leave it to the sole leopard shifter on the team to pick up on such things. "It's just been a rough few days is all. Nothing exciting." As much as he wanted to spill the beans to someone, he didn't dare. The last thing he needed was for word to get back to Tucker. The poor guy had enough on his plate right now without additional stress. *Although he seems to have found a way to work off the tension and pretty damn fast.* The snarky remark in his head made the sting hurt that much more.

"Interesting." Mack took the menu from the waitress, glanced over it, then told her what he wanted. She darted toward the kitchen once again. "Tucker is in a fit after losing his starting spot and you're sulking and antisocial."

"So?"

"So, it seems coincidental that you two were chummy at the party, left together, and have been up in arms since." Mack stared at him intensely.

Damn it. If Mack knows, then how many of the others do as well?

Dixon steeled himself behind his poker face. "I didn't see you at the party." He turned the tables, hoping to divert the topic and Mack's interest off track.

Mack grinned ruefully. "People only see me when I want them to."

The comment made Dixon blink. "Meaning you're lurking around in the shadows and spying on others?"

Mack shrugged, then took a long drink of his water. He lowered the glass and met Dixon's gaze. "People watching is a hobby after all."

"Uh-huh." Dixon took a drink while studying the man across the table. "Curiosity killed the cat," he warned.

Mack had joined the team last year. Nowhere near a rookie, the seasoned veteran had spent time with a handful of teams. His sage advice and easygoing manner fit in well with the Predators. Normally quiet, he had a penchant for stirring the pot now and again. However, with Trigger on the team to keep people on their toes, Mack's version of mischief largely went unnoticed. Until now.

Dixon saw the predator inside Mack as well as the stereotypical inquisitiveness felines tended to possess. The combination added up for a bad mixture in Dixon's present frame of mind.

"So says the fox." Mack smirked.

A minute passed in silence before Mack struck up the conversation again. "Maybe I should tell you what I think and you can tell me if I'm wrong." He leaned forward and pitched his voice low. "I think you and Tucker hooked up after the party. Now, there's regrets. That's why he's inviting women into his hotel room right and left, why he's avoiding you when you two used to be close buddies. Tucker's wound tight. You're edgy and ready to blow."

Dixon's lips parted at the spot-on summing up of the situation. "And how did you deduce all that?"

Mack's face eased as a small smile appeared on his lips. "Like I said, I people watch. Besides, it wasn't hard to piece together. Especially when you both still carried each other's scent the next day. Subtle, but there."

"Here I thought canines had the market cornered on great noses." Dixon snorted.

Mack's smile grew. "Not even close, buddy." He sobered a little. "What are you going to do about Tucker?"

"I don't know." The truth poured out.

Sympathy flashed in Mack's eyes. "You want him, but he's resisting."

"More like running."

"Then you'll just have to catch him."

Dixon snorted. "Easier said than done."

Mack appraised him for a long moment. "You're smart. Give it some time and you'll come up with a plan."

"I wish I had your optimism."

"It'll happen. Just you wait and see."

The certainty in Mack's voice sparked Dixon's interest. "How can you be so sure?"

"Simple. I observe and I scent. Tucker might be keeping his distance, but he's not forgotten you."

"I hope you're right."

"Always am." Mack gave a quick nod, then turned to the waitress who'd just arrived with their meal.

Dixon clung to his prediction and hope flared the tiniest bit. *Maybe, just maybe, this can still work out.*

Just like pigs can sprout wings and fly.

Chapter 6

OPENING DAY. One of the greatest events in baseball. The beginning of the season, when everyone is undefeated and all teams have high hopes of going all the way. Fans pour into the stadiums, eager to celebrate another year of remarkable plays, amazing happenings, grand slams, and the underdog rising to victory. It all started with this one day.

And I'm sitting on the fucking bench.

Tucker ran his hand through his hair, then replaced the cap on his head. This day had been one of the highlights of his years playing the game. Yet, for the first time ever, he wasn't on the field or taking his turn in the batter's box. Instead, a rookie filled in his spot.

Not my spot any longer.

He grouched to himself, irritable and depressed with his life at the moment. First, he'd been demoted to a backup role. Yeah, he deserved it after the way he played during the preseason. He didn't argue with Banner's logic. Not in the least. The result still left him hanging and with more doubts that he'd ever encountered before. Could he make it back? Did he even want to try? Maybe this was how good players finished their careers, slowly sliding down the scale until they threw in the towel and quit. But he'd never considered life without baseball and hadn't ever given a second job another thought. Which left him between a rock and a hard place—either step it up or expect to hang out in the dugout as an observer for most of the games.

Dixon jumped into the air to catch a ball, hit hard and right at him. Easily, he gloved it, pulled it out with his free hand, and threw it back to Graham, the pitcher.

Dixon. Tucker couldn't get the guy out of his mind since the morning after they fell into bed with one another. He'd been rattled, still was, and ended up being an ass to Dixon. Not that he saw any other choice in the matter. What happened between them couldn't be repeated. No way. Besides, he didn't want Dixon getting the wrong idea.

What wrong idea? You begged him to fuck you. He chastised himself with the blunt truth.

Just a onetime fuck and it was out of his system. *For good.*

Liar.

Tucker growled at his inner beast. As much as he tried to smooth things over with excuses, his animal side disagreed. To the wild dog, everything was black and white. Unfortunately, in the real world of humans and shifters, gray existed all over the place.

Like right now with the whole mess of a straight man going home with a gay one, stripping down, and getting it on. He wasn't into men. Never had been and never would be. Considering that, he knew to lead Dixon on with a little bit of hope would only prolong the inevitable. He liked the guy. As a teammate and friend. That's it. No friends with benefits and certainly nothing more serious.

That's the way it had to be. He'd make sure of it. Because that's all he knew. The thought of things changing now proved too overwhelming to even think about.

My life sucks.

Oddly enough, until a couple of days ago, he thought he was cruising along just fine. Then the first bump in the road led to the second bigger pitfall. Now, he found himself benched, confused, and pretty damn lost.

And sick of spending every waking hour fixating on what happened.

"Hey, Tucker. How's it going?" Milo, one of the relief outfielders, strolled the length of the seats.

Just fucking fantastic. Tucker dutifully bobbed his head. "Good and you?"

"Can't complain. Another season, another chance to collect another championship trophy." He kept going all the way to the cooler, grabbed a bottle of water, then retraced his steps. Standing next to the entrance to the dugout, Milo seemed content to watch the game without the annoyance of the railing being in his line of vision.

The crack of the bat drew Tucker's attention.

Dixon dove to his left, caught the ball, then jumped back to his feet and fired a laser to first base in time to beat the runner.

Damn, he's good.

Tucker raked Dixon's body with his gaze. *And damn fine looking too.*

He listened to his own words and cringed. Pretty hard to pretend nothing happened when he caught himself ogling Dixon. That had to stop. Immediately.

After yet another quick self-lecture, he focused on the game.

Graham struck out the next player before trotting to the dugout. Sweat beaded his face and stained his shirt already.

Tucker felt for the guy. As a polar bear shifter, Graham didn't handle the heat as well as some others, namely himself. Built for the African plains, he reveled in the summer temperatures.

The rest of the players came in from the field right after the battery, each one either finding a spot on the bench, heading for the water, or simply dropping their gloves off, strapping on a helmet, and grabbing a bat. Dixon among them.

Trigger stripped his catcher's gear except for his shin guards, grabbed two bottles of water and passed one to Graham.

The softness in Trigger's eyes as he looked at his mate made Tucker's heart kick against his ribs. Even a surly old cuss like Trigger could find a mate. The fact gave hope to others.

Except Tucker. He wanted no part of that business. Much better to love them and leave them than to settle down and play house for a lifetime. No commitment, no getting burned and abandoned at some point when things got tough.

Dixon flicked his attention to Tucker, opened his mouth, then shut it right back.

Tucker avoided eye contact, stood, and moved to the far end of the bench. Less chance of being face-to-face with Dixon that way. Avoidance became the goal. *At least for now.*

Two men headed right back to the field. Dixon was one of them. He strode directly for the warm-up circle, making a few practice swings as soon as he arrived.

Dixon was the progeny of two generations of professional baseball players, both of whom had been at the top of the league in hitting during their careers. He'd followed in their footsteps. He earned a nice batting average each year and always proved to be a hit with the fans of the team. Right on cue, cheers and applause broke out, even among those supporting the opponents, as Dixon walked to the batter's box.

What would that be like?

Tucker, having been raised with nothing, couldn't fathom life as a kid born with a silver spoon. No having to try to hold down a job flipping burgers while attending school and playing ball. No walking to practice because his mother had a shift at the diner and couldn't be there. No wearing ragged and torn clothes because the budget didn't allow anything new unless it came from the thrift store a couple of times per year.

He shook his head in disbelief at how two lives could be so opposite, yet they ended up in the same place. A bit of envy invaded his thoughts as Dixon took his cuts at pitches. Dixon had a built-in coach and ample time to practice growing up. He'd been destined for stardom from a young age.

So unlike me.

The reminder of where he'd come from and what he'd been through acted like a lightning rod for Tucker. He'd lived a version of hell and never lost sight of his goal in life. The way out of poverty revolved around the game. Hard work, extra hours. Anything and everything to get just a hair better.

I'll make it work. I just have to.

Dixon laid off a low slider, stepped out of the box, and lightly smacked his bat against his cleats to get the dirt out of them.

The guy who breathed baseball, knew the ins and outs, with all the right moves, stood just a few feet away, preparing to show everyone exactly why his reputation as a ball player shone bright.

Built-in coach. Practice time. Words replayed through his mind as he studied Dixon's technique. *Maybe if I had such a thing....*

Two foul balls and three balls later, Dixon made solid contact, sending a looper into shallow center field for a base hit.

Nicely done. Tucker gave credit where credit was due.

Lance entered the box next. The tiger shifter rookie had the size and the strength to play at this level. The question became could he hold up under the pressure, especially when playing against this level of skill day in and day out.

As if he heard Tucker's internal questions, Lance swung at the first pitch. The loud crack drew everyone's eyes first to the batter, then upward where the ball sailed high and long, finally landing in the left field stands several rows back.

Lance, with a grin on his face, accepted a high five from Banner at third base as he jogged the rest of the way home.

Tucker applauded Lance. He'd proven himself, all right. There was no denying the rookie had plenty of talent and enough gumption to last.

I've got one hell of a battle on my hands.

With that realization, Tucker started thinking of ways to get back to the top of his game and earn his spot back. The alternative was too damn possible and downright demoralizing.

TUCKER STEPPED out of the shower and finished towel drying his hair before tossing the damp cloth into a nearby hamper. He grabbed his boxers and slipped them on, shivering a little at the difference in temperature from the hot water to the air in his room. While brushing his teeth, he absently made a mental note to check the thermostat, then moved on to the task of combing his hair. Task done, he returned to the living area of his hotel room. The old place across from the stadium had been restored recently to mimic the days of grandeur. All the décor reminded him of the Roaring Twenties, including the Art Nouveau pictures with various geographic designs and vague depictions, and the beige walls with light orange curtains. Not his favorite color combos, but the brightness added a touch of class. He'd give them credit for thinking outside the box, anyway.

He checked the clock and found the hands closing in on midnight. The drawback when one played night games. By the time they left the park and returned either home or to a hotel, the wee hours of the next morning were normally upon them. Tucker didn't mind in the least. Unlike a handful of the other players, he preferred to stay up half the night and sleep in the next morning. Much easier to adapt to than the other way around. His wild cousins hunted at all hours of the day. Thankfully, he didn't have to follow their schedule. Although having the support of a family pack would be nice.

Wild dogs were very social and nearly always lived in groups. To be alone was rare and probably a recipe for a short lifespan. While shifters differed from their wild cousins, some instincts and habits carried over. Namely the need for companionship. Something Tucker really hadn't had a steady supply of until lately.

And if I don't get my head out of my ass, I won't have that luxury for long.

He walked over, adjusted the thermostat once more, and sat down on the couch. Automatically, he picked up the remote control and started channel surfing. The nightly ritual helped him settle down for a good night's sleep.

His phone rang. He plucked it off the couch cushion and checked the caller ID. His mother. *Just great.* Most people would panic at calls being so late at night. With his schedule, he'd be much more upset if someone called him at seven a.m. rather than now.

Since she seldom made contact, he went ahead and answered. "Hi, Mom."

"Tucker. How are you?"

She started all their conversations the very same way. He grinned slightly despite the emptiness he felt when she checked on him. In all these years, he couldn't find enough forgiveness for the woman for abandoning him and returning to the pack when he entered college. That single move left him totally on his own and alone.

At least she did that much, his inner animal pointed out.

Ignoring the comment, he went with the flow, keeping the discussion casual and vague. "Fine. Busy. The usual."

"Nothing going on?" A hint of concern mixed with curiosity came through loud and clear.

His internal radar pinged and his breath caught. She knew something, but what, he didn't dare guess. "Nope. Nothing." He forced a bit of boredom into his tone.

"Then why didn't you play today? It's opening day. You *always* play on opening day."

He grimaced. "It's no big deal."

"Are you injured?"

"No, Mom. I'm just fine." The thought of her prying and nagging irritated him. He paused a second to debate telling her the truth. If he didn't she'd pester him until he gave in. Not something he wanted to deal with right now. Honesty won out. "A rookie earned my starting position is all. I'm riding the bench in the backup role. Just until I get back into the flow of the game this season."

Silence followed.

"Are you okay with that?" Her question came across tentatively.

"Well, yes and no. It's not like I'm going to beat the guy up because he's young, hungry, and talented. But I'm working hard to prove that I'm the better player."

He added optimism and an upbeat attitude into his voice. The last thing he wanted was to sound like a whiny spoiled brat. After all, the buck stopped with him.

"When will that be?"

"I don't know. When the manager makes that decision, I guess." He stretched out his legs and crossed them at the ankles. "It's not a big deal. This happens all the time."

"Mostly due to injury, but you said that wasn't the case," she pointed out.

He sighed.

"You've been in a slump as of late. Both in hitting and fielding." She made the words a statement.

"How did you know?"

She snorted. "Tucker Wilde. I might not be at your games, but I do keep up with you. The games on television, I watch or record if I'm not able to be at home. And I do check the team's website quite often."

He blinked as realization struck. She followed his career. One way or another. "Why?" The question slipped out.

"Why what? Why do I check on you? Why do I read everything I can find about you and watch you on television?"

"Well, yeah. You were all too in a hurry to get back to the pack." *And abandon me in the process.* Old hurt trickled through.

"Tucker, you're my son. What else would I do but watch you play baseball? Learn about your life and what's happening in it? That's what mothers do when it comes to their kids."

He rubbed his free hand over his face. The mini lecture went over like a lead balloon. Just like most of their conversations. "Forget I said anything."

"No. I'm not going to forget it. You don't get it, do you?"

He blew out a breath in frustration. "Look, Mom. I've got to go. I'll catch you later."

"Tucker—"

"Later, Mom." He clicked off the call before she could say anything more.

This must be the week of asshole-hood for him. First, he'd told Dixon that their coupling meant nothing, obviously stabbing the guy in the heart. Now, he'd hung up on his mother rather than argue about her getting involved in his life from afar and years down the road from abandoning him.

"Yeah, I'm not going to win the kind and caring person of the year award any time soon." He rested his head on the back of the couch and stared at the ceiling.

My life definitely sucks.

Nowhere to go but up, right? He only wished he could believe that would be the case.

Frustrated with the whole day, Tucker made an impulsive decision. He hurried over to his suitcase, pulled out a pair of slacks and a silk shirt, and tugged them on. After a final check in the mirror, he slipped on his loafers, tucked his wallet in his pocket, and headed out the door. A night of hot bodies at a nearby club would surely help. If nothing else, he could put away a couple of drinks or get up close and personal with a lovely young lady. Either one would brighten things up in his world.

No sooner had Tucker stepped out of the main lobby doors than he caught a glimpse of Dixon. Only he wasn't alone.

Dixon walked next to another guy, this one with light-colored hair, dressed in jeans and a button-down shirt. Good looking, the man had a smile on his face, which only widened when Dixon whispered to him. They had their arms around one another and were heading toward the side entrance of the building. Since Dixon would have a key card, he didn't have to bring his newfound date through the front doors for all to see.

As they continued on, Tucker saw Dixon cup the other man's rear and give it a squeeze.

He recalled what Dixon's touch on his own ass felt like, and awareness hit him square in the chest.

The thought of Dixon screwing another man stirred up both hurt and anger. He couldn't say anything. After all, he'd walked out and pretty much told Dixon that their time together was equivalent to a faux pas and easily forgettable. But, seeing that Dixon moved on to another hookup changed things.

What do I expect? Dixon to sit at home every night pining away? Of course he was going to find a new man. Shifters were a randy bunch after all. Dixon would be no different, seeking out another guy for sex. For companionship. Maybe even something more permanent. *Something more than he has with me, that's for damn sure.*

Just like I did with that woman as soon as we arrived at the hotel. Trying to regain a firm hold on being straight, I pretty much shoved it in Dixon's face. Regret rested heavily on his shoulders. He now knew how it felt—like he'd been replaced for not making the grade. The sting would last, that he understood.

Seeing Dixon with another man cleared the murky waters a little. While still a bit hesitant, Tucker knew he had to either step up to the plate with Dixon or to wave him good-bye forever.

If only I knew which path to follow.

His interest in going out fizzled. Peace and quiet in the hotel room while watching some television appealed more.

With one final glance at the couple, Tucker turned on his heel and retraced his steps.

Chapter 7

DIXON HEADED to the plate for his turn at batting practice. Tucker passed him by in the opposite direction but didn't even bother to make eye contact as he went.

The silent jab irritated Dixon and dug at his still-raw feelings.

It had been that way for two weeks now. Ever since Tucker declared their time together was a drunken mistake. No matter what Dixon tried, Tucker eluded him. At his wit's end, Dixon pretty much gave up on that particular dream. Unfortunately, he seemed to have lost a friend in the process.

No use crying over spilled milk or one-night stands gone bad.

He dug his cleats into the dirt, bent his knees, and assumed his stance. A couple of beats later, he swung the bat, made contact, then promptly cussed as the ball arced into deep left field. The third fly ball in a row. Not a good outing, even for batting practice. The pregame ritual used to relax him, get his mind on track for the upcoming game. Now, it seemed to be just another thorn in his side.

"If you'd quit dropping that shoulder like I told you, you wouldn't be popping up."

The all too familiar voice made Dixon cringe. He turned to see his father standing near the warm-up circle, a stern look pasted on his face.

Well, hell. Did he really have to show up here? Right now? Like I don't have enough issues at the moment.

He spared his father a glance. "Dad. I wasn't expecting you."

"Thought I might drop by and see if we can correct a thing or two. Your stats aren't as good as they could be."

"Whose ever is?" he uttered under his breath. "Three-fifty isn't anything to sneeze at." He turned his attention back to the mound where one of the assistant coaches threw out grapefruits for the players to hit.

Terrance approached with his chin up and shoulders back. A self-confident carriage if Dixon ever saw one. His father knew he'd been big stuff and still was to this day. That certainly hadn't changed.

"By the time I was your age, I owned the hitting records."

Dixon lowered his bat and swung around. "Guess what, Dad. I'm not you." He didn't realize he'd growled loudly until nearby players jerked around to stare at him. The sound also caught Banner's attention, and he frowned in Dixon's direction.

"You're my kid. I expect better. You could match my average if you'd just try a little harder and take some advice from a pro." Terrance stopped near the batter's box and bit out the retort with restrained anger.

"Lucky me." Sarcasm dripped from the words.

Terrance scowled, his lips pulled back to show his fangs. A sure sign of growing frustration and agitation. "You'll show respect. I earned it. Every bit of it."

"I didn't say you didn't, Dad, but how about backing off and letting me play as I see fit?" Dixon fired right back. He threw his bat to the ground and fisted his hands. A low rumble inside his head told exactly what his inner beast thought about the situation. As it was, he held the reins of control with an iron grip, for fear his fox half would break free and go on a rampage against his own father.

Some instincts were firmly lodged inside a shifter's genetic makeup, despite their human parts. Protectiveness, defense of those he cares for, and standing up to a challenge from another male existed at the top of the list.

"I would if you would actually play up to your capability. Laziness and slacking doesn't leave a bright mark on the family name. I worked hard to keep the name as one of the best in baseball, just like my father before me. And, you'll do the same." Terrance finished loudly and with command.

Fur is going to fly. Dixon opened his mouth to tell his father off, only to be cut off.

"Mr. Foxx. I was hoping I'd get to meet you one day. Tucker Wilde." Tucker walked up quickly with his hand held out.

Terrance shook it. "Good to meet you."

Tucker smiled at him. "Hey, do you think you could autograph my bat? I'd appreciate it." He handed over the bat. "I have a place of honor for it. Only the best for the greatest player of our time."

The pinched expression faded as Terrance smiled at the lavish praise. "Sure. Got a pen?"

"Yep." Tucker held one out.

Dixon watched the interaction with puzzlement. In all the time they'd played together, he couldn't recall Tucker asking about getting an autograph from his father. Hell, he couldn't even remember them talking about his father at all. Which made the scene all that more confusing.

Tucker glanced up, met Dixon's gaze, and winked.

Dixon gave a brief nod as the puzzle pieces fell into place. Whether Tucker really sought the souvenir was a moot point. He'd intervened to spare Dixon and to prevent the argument threatening to blow out of proportion in full public view.

"Thank you," he mouthed.

Tucker inclined his head before turning back to Terrance.

Banner nudged Dixon toward the dugout. "Enough batting practice for the day. We have a team meeting in five. Get going." He looked over at Tucker. "You too."

"Yes, sir." Tucker grinned at Terrance once more. "Thanks."

"Welcome."

Dixon didn't waste time. He made a beeline for the dugout and didn't look back. The far end of the bench was empty and called his name. He sat down and brooded over his situation. His father would never be happy with his play. No matter how hard he tried, he'd never live up to expectations. *So why bother?*

Right then and there, Dixon vowed to never give a damn about his father's opinion ever again. To do otherwise would only decay his sanity and put him on the warpath whenever his father showed up. Better to just let it go and move on than to have an all-out fight in fox form on the field. And that's what it was coming to. Would have happened today if Tucker hadn't stepped in.

All well and good except the fury hadn't left his body and the pregame antics stole his focus, only sending his mood further into the doldrums. *A hell of a start to a game with nowhere to go but up.*

Two hours later he found himself right back on the bench, the exact same spot he'd plopped down at before the game started. Before, he'd needed a break in order to simmer down from the near altercation with his father. This time, he'd been replaced in the game due to poor play and bad temper. Zero for three at bats and two errors charged to him. He'd mouthed off at the ump over a couple of strikes and threw his glove down in the dirt in a fit when a runner had been called safe after Dixon tagged him just before the guy slid into base. While that was awful enough of a showing, it was worse since the game was only in the fourth inning.

He'd kicked at the dirt, tossed his glove to the bench, and glared at those around him. Though not their fault in the least, he didn't feel up to chatting. Better to warn the others away rather than say something to piss them off as well.

So much for going up.

"If you'd get your head in the game, then you'd still be out there." Trigger leaned against the railing of the dugout and crossed his arms over his chest. "Drop everything at the door next time."

Dixon saw red. "You fucking know-it-all." He stood up.

Trigger arched an eyebrow, seemingly not the least bit intimidated. He didn't have to be, as he had more than enough muscles and mass to pound Dixon into a puddle.

Still, Dixon wasn't backing down. He'd had enough of people telling him what to do lately. Enough was enough.

"I'll let you in on a little secret. People do shit like what happened today to get into your mind and mess up your game. Congratulations. You fell into that trap." He dropped his hands to his sides. "Next time, remember that you're in the big leagues for a reason. Do what you do and to hell with anyone else."

Oddly enough, Trigger's words hit a chord with Dixon. The anger evaporated, leaving irritation and annoyance in its wake. "What do you know about it?"

Trigger grinned slightly. "I grew up with four older brothers. I know all about mind games, beatings, and sucker punches." With that said, he ambled down the way toward the cooler filled with water bottles.

Dixon saw Trigger in a new light. Sure, the big guy was an asshole most of the time, but perhaps he had a reason to be. *Survival of the fittest and all that.*

A LOW growl followed by a grunt carried to Dixon's ears. He pulled up the sides of the pillow in hopes of drowning out the noise.

He'd been thrilled to have a hotel room by himself. The luxury happened now and again, about half of the away games, players had to double up. He'd been lucky enough to fall into the category of having a room to himself. That had worked out well for him, or so he thought. Unfortunately, his room was bracketed by the two mated couples on the team. Wiley and Ram had the one to the left while Graham and Trigger occupied the space to the right. All fine and good until both sides started getting frisky.

And Dixon's advanced hearing and nose picked up on everything. *Damn it, anyway.*

The unmistakable squeak of a bed added into the mix of sexual sounds.

What the hell is wrong with people tonight? The Florida warmth sending everyone into heat? Or the annual breeding season is starting right now?

Dixon groaned as the ruckus continued.

In truth, he couldn't begrudge them their pleasure. If things had worked out differently, he'd be doing the exact same thing—with Tucker. The possibilities flew through his mind, making him horny and beyond frustrated.

Though he'd hooked up with a guy from a club recently, the night of hardcore sex did little to appease his rampant libido. The man had been a looker and a great lay, but Dixon's heart wasn't into it, still too fixated on the one man who he wanted above all else, but couldn't have.

Time heals all wounds. I just wish it would hurry up.

A sharp yip from one of the rooms sealed the deal.

Dixon got up, threw on some clothes and shoes before leaving the room. He needed space, air, and somewhere quiet. As he stepped out the front door of the hotel, the lights from the stadium across the street drew him. The two security guards gave him a friendly nod and let him pass without a hassle.

Automatically, he strode onto the diamond and took his time looking around. The empty stands suited his mood, as did the vacant field. For the life of him, he couldn't recall the last time he stepped out on the infield because he loved the game. Nothing more complicated than that. Since childhood, it had been his father's obsession and the only way to please the man.

Goes to show some things never change. He snorted to himself.

Lately, he'd begun to wonder if the high stakes were worth it. The traveling, the pressure, the demands. Where did his happiness fit into the equation?

When no answer came, he sauntered toward the stands, climbed over the railing, and took a seat in the front row near his home spot of third base.

What a hell of a shitty mess this last twenty-four hours has been. First, Mack opened a can of worms at dinner last night. Then, his father invaded batting practice and tore him apart for his technique and lack of solidly hit balls. After that, his outing in the game royally sucked. Now, it's screwing time at the hotel of lust and he'd been left out.

He propped his feet up on the center metal bar of the railing, folded his arms over his chest, and simply stared out over the field in search of answers to the silent questions.

A shadow fell across the first base line. Dixon turned to find another man heading his way.

He noticed the walk and the body build a second before his olfactory senses picked up on the unique scent of the individual.

Tucker.

His heart picked up speed as his breath caught in his chest.

A second later, he recalled the issues of late and checked his excitement. Tucker couldn't be here searching for him. Instead, he'd probably made a date for some kinky hookup with a woman in the dugout or some such nonsense. *Something I damn well don't want to bear witness to.* Even his bid at a quiet night couldn't come true.

With a sigh of dejection, Dixon stood and turned to leave.

"Wait. Don't go."

The quiet words stopped Dixon. He swiveled, caught the sadness on Tucker's face, and sat back down. Nothing about the man's body language spoke of sex or a randy shifter on the prowl. Instead, Tucker reminded him of a guy who'd lost his best friend. Dixon's heart tugged at the thought.

Tucker climbed the stairs, stopped at the same level, then made his way over. He took the seat next to Dixon, folded his hands together, and stared out over the empty diamond.

For a long moment, neither spoke. The silence wasn't uncomfortable, but it did fill Dixon with an odd type of tension. Words left him completely.

"It's been a hell of a season so far." Tucker's soft voice carried plenty of lackluster energy as well as some self-reproach. "I can't get back into the game. It's like the fire has blown out and I'm just going through the motions."

Dixon empathized. His fire had burned out eons ago.

"I deserved to lose my starting spot. Only now, I don't know how to get it back."

"The question is, do you want to?" Dixon uttered the query he'd asked himself dozens of times.

Tucker lifted his head and gazed over to Dixon. "Yeah, I do. Baseball is my life. My outlet. The only thing that keeps me going."

"That's a lot of pressure to excel at a sport that's supposed to be fun," Dixon pointed out.

Tucker sighed and turned his attention to the field once again. "Yeah, but it's always been that way. Baseball was my ticket out. I guess it still is."

"Out of where?"

TUCKER TOOK a second to decide how to answer Dixon's question. "Banner asked if there were any problems at home that could serve as a distraction." Tucker discovered that since he'd started talking, he needed to air everything out. Dixon made for a great friend, until Tucker screwed things up that one night, and a good listener, so he kept going.

"Are there?" Dixon asked.

"Hard to have family issues when you have no family," Tucker quietly answered.

Dixon's mouth fell open. "I don't understand." Confusion covered his face and laced his words.

Tucker glanced away, unable to bear witness to the expression of pity sure to come. "My mother and I were exiled when she had me." Actually, that wasn't entirely accurate. He'd been banished, not his mother as evidenced by the fact she'd returned to the wild dog pack the same day she'd dropped him off at college as an eighteen-year-old kid. His father had never been in the picture. Good or bad, Tucker couldn't really say. "She toughed it out until move in day at the university. I'd earned a full-ride college baseball scholarship. She was relieved, I think. Anyway, she let me out at my dorm, dropped the bombshell that she was going back to the pack, and drove off. I stood there, suitcase in hand, and watched her go. I knew that I'd been abandoned just like an unwanted puppy at an animal shelter."

He heard a gasp from Dixon but didn't respond. He couldn't. Not when memories flooded to the fore.

I've done my duty by you. Now go make something of yourself.

Mom?

I'm going back to the pack, Tucker. Starting over.

Without me. The words remained unspoken, but he'd read the situation clearly enough. Along with everyone else, she considered him disposable and unworthy. Just because of his mixed genetics.

The old wound still stung.

From that day forward, he threw himself into baseball and never looked back.

"Tucker?"

Dixon's voice drew him from the painful past.

"Care to tell me why?" Dixon twisted a little to stare at him.

"I'm not full-blooded." Tucker whispered the words.

"Could have fooled me."

"My father was a hybrid. I'm three-quarters wild dog."

"And?" Dixon persisted.

"One-quarter domesticated dog." Shame reared its ugly head. Tucker drew in air. "Because of that, the pack doesn't recognize me as one of them." He focused on his intertwined hands resting on his lap. "Hybrids aren't accepted, period. A domestic dog shifter, even purebred, doesn't even rank *that* high in treatment."

"I've seen your shifted form. You look just like a wild dog, including all the patches of blond and white over the black coat. I especially like the tuft of bright white at the tip of your tail." Dixon grinned.

Tucker halfheartedly smiled. "I guess in that respect, I'm lucky. My father's mix was wild dog with a Catahoula leopard dog. Lots of spots in both breeds along with a similar build." Tucker peered over at Dixon. "They would have put me to death or abandoned me to the elements were it a couple of centuries ago." Insight began to surface in his mind, making him see his mother in a new light.

"But now?"

Tucker shrugged. "My mother hid me away. Raised me as a single mother the best she could, I guess, especially without the luxury of support of any kind from anyone."

He recalled the tough times and his shoulders slumped. His mother could have dropped him off at a hospital, an orphanage, entered him into foster care and returned home where she'd have a much easier life. Instead, she toughed it out for all those years. He'd fixated on her departure, not on her sticking with him.

"I hated her for leaving me. Abandoning me. But now...."

"You see the sacrifices she made to get you through to college?"

"Yeah. I received a baseball scholarship. She was thrilled. Relieved. I didn't understand at the time, but I do now. She longed for her family but needed me on my own in order to go back. So, I guess when I entered college, she was free."

"Pretty damn sad if you ask me." Dixon's eyes reflected sympathy along with respect.

Both bolstered Tucker's confidence a smidgen.

"Forcing a young mother to make such choices in life. That's bullshit." The strong words were laced with indignation.

"It's reality," Tucker answered without malice. The pack's philosophy wasn't going to change anytime soon. Yet, he could finally understand more about his mother and her own brand of courage once he looked past his own selfishness. Maybe he had reason to be angry, hurt, and upset, but one action didn't a life make. He'd chosen to focus on the bad times instead of facing facts. She'd given up a lot for him and done the best she could, considering the circumstances. Not every wild dog shifter would have done half of what she did in trying to raise him.

Dixon blew out a breath, the momentary anger seeming to recede just as quickly as it appeared. "Do you still speak with your mother? Visit her?"

"Talk now and again is all." He really hadn't missed her in the beginning. His anger clouded his feelings. Now, he had a great urge to call her up and hash things out. Especially after being such an ass the last time they spoke.

Dixon tilted his head. "Why do I have a feeling things weren't easy for you and your mother?"

"Probably because they weren't." Tucker leaned back against the plastic backrest of the seat. "She only had a high school education. Her job prospects were limited. Money was a luxury we didn't have." He recalled all the nights he went to bed hungry and realized that his mother did so more than he. In all honesty, he'd never thought about it much, but saw all those dinners that she prepared but never partook of. Instead, she talked to him about his day as he ate.

Guilt settled on his shoulders, the weight pushing them down. "She gave so much to me and I hated her for leaving. How could I have been so blind?"

Dixon reached out, then settled for placing his hand on the armrest. "Because you were a kid, first. Secondly, you were hurt. Angry. The pain of abandonment colored your view. It's normal and to be expected."

"I'm a fucking prick." Tucker sighed heavily and looked to the heavens.

"You're human. Well, part of you is." Dixon grinned without humor.

"If you say so," Tucker answered tiredly. He took a moment to appraise Dixon. "You never told me about your childhood."

Dixon glanced around the stadium. "It wasn't what it was cracked up to be. As evidenced by that debacle of a batting practice today."

Intrigued, Tucker swiveled to catch the expressions on Dixon's face as he told his story. "It can't be worse than mine."

Dixon snorted. "There's no trophy for who had the worst life, you know."

"True. So, tell me already."

"Everyone knows my father, idolizes him."

Tucker nodded. "Terrance Foxx. Hall of Famer. One of the best hitters in the league. Got his autograph on a bat to show it off."

"Yeah, his lists of achievements go on and on. Too bad he wasn't half the father as he was a ball player."

"Such a pompous ass who showed up today to cut his own son to ribbons in public because he feels you're not living up to his expectations." Tucker didn't mince words and his tone spoke volumes filled with ire and irritation.

"I grew up knowing one thing—baseball. He was going to turn me into a professional player one way or the other. Just like his father did with him." Dixon rubbed at his chin. "I had private coaches. Practice every day of my life. An indoor park if rain shut down the outdoor ones. Money could buy all those things, certainly. Only it couldn't buy my father's love. He didn't care about my wants, dreams, or wishes. I won a ribbon in the junior high science project competition. I knew he'd be proud. When I showed it to him, he just shook his head, tossed the ribbon over his shoulder, and dragged me to the batting cages."

"Ouch."

"Yeah." Dixon blew out a breath. "I guess I do owe my career to him."

There was something in Dixon's voice that sparked Tucker's curiosity. "Do you even like playing the game?"

Dixon shifted his gaze sideways enough to meet Tucker's eyes. "I'm really not sure. It's all I've ever known."

"Damn." Tucker understood Dixon so much better. The guy, though wealthy, tended to live like an average person. All the benefits of growing up with a silver spoon in his mouth made him wish for something else. Normalcy. A father's love that didn't revolve around a baseball diamond.

"We're quite a pair," Dixon said.

Tucker grinned slightly. "You can say that again. Pretty damn pitiful, if you ask me. You had all the money and fame growing up but couldn't buy the one thing you wanted most. I grew up in pretty dire poverty, dreaming of the fame and fortune that came with a contract to play in the big leagues."

"You're out to prove something. That you belong."

"And you're still trying to please your father." Tucker saw the writing on the wall. Dixon played the game because the only way to impress his father was to succeed on the field. He highly doubted Dixon truly loved the game. How could he? Tucker eyed Dixon. "Where does that leave us?"

Dixon stared at him, hope and a latent fire broadcasting clearly in his eyes. "I don't know."

A flicker of desire lit in Tucker's gut. He so wanted to give in, but couldn't. Not yet. Not with his life turned upside down. Right now, he needed his friend more than a casual fuck.

"Maybe we can find our way back to the game. Together."

Dixon nodded slowly. "I'd like that."

"Me too."

"Dixon...." Tucker started to say more, but his courage faltered.

"It's enough." Dixon clapped him on the shoulder.

Relieved, Tucker shot him a grateful smile. "We can do this."

"Yep. We'll flash some glove and hit a few out of the park. Once we get back on track, the rest will follow."

The rest of what? Tucker didn't have the guts to ask. Instead, he threw caution to the wind and opted to go with the flow. A new approach, but one that appeared quite promising.

Chapter 8

"Stu Simpson is pitching today. What do you know about him?" Dixon asked as he opened the door of the nearest batting cage located under the stands.

Tucker stepped inside with bat in hand. He pulled up what he'd observed about the guy in his mind, compliments of their batting coach who consistently handed out a page or two of condensed need-to-know information on the likely pitchers they'd face in the upcoming game. The guy gave a verbal rundown during batting practice as well, but expected his players to read over the provided guide.

"Likes to throw fast balls."

"Yep. And a mean backdoor curve." Dixon walked behind the machine and turned some buttons. "I've got this set for both fastballs and curve balls. It'll give you a fair idea of what you'll face with Stu."

Tucker nodded. He had no clue if he was going to play today, but he'd made a commitment to fight for his spot. That meant being ready for anything.

The first ball flew by. He swung and missed by a mile. "Damn. What's that set on? Two hundred miles per hour?"

Dixon grinned. "One hundred and ten actually."

"Shit." Tucker resumed his stance and waited. The next ball came slower but moved away from him. Tucker swung and managed to get a piece of it.

"There you go. Fight off the pitches. Stu is tricky. If he can get the ump to call those lower ones, he'll be having a hay day. Best to just foul them off and wait for a better pitch."

"Yeah." Tucker felt like he was back in college and his batting coach preached details as Tucker made his cuts. Not a bad reminder since he'd learned tons of stuff from the old man.

He spared a quick glance at Dixon. The guy knew his stuff. His father, while an ass, passed down his knowledge over the years, helping mold Dixon into a great hitter. As far as batting coaches went, Dixon would make an excellent one when he decided to turn in his playing glove.

He focused on the machine, saw a fastball coming hard, and unloaded. It slammed against the back fence with force.

He grinned. "That felt good. Really good."

"Looked great too. Nice motion and follow-through." Dixon added some more baseballs to the machine from a nearby basket. "You've got a natural flow, just need the time and room to extend."

"So the back of the batter's box for Stu, huh?" Feeling more chipper, Tucker rolled his shoulders and prepared for the next pitch.

"Definitely." Dixon looked up. "Ready?"

"Yeah."

The next ball headed his direction. Tucker hit it square. Same with the next one and the one after that. A dozen more pitches came with Tucker making contact each time.

"Nice." Dixon came around to the entry gate, let himself in, and patted Tucker on the shoulder. "How does it feel now?"

"Great." Tucker grinned with confidence. "Really good. Like there's hope."

"There was never a doubt of that." Dixon stared at him for a long moment.

Tucker read the pride as well as the happiness in Dixon's eyes. A spark of longing flared for a quick second. Not ready to deal with that side of their relationship, Tucker focused on the present.

"Your turn." He handed the bat over and left the cage. A few strides later, he stood at the back of the pitching machine, assessed the options, and smiled wickedly to himself. He cranked the speed up to the highest setting. "You ready?"

"Bring it on."

Tucker hit the button, and Dixon swung with all his might, only to fan at the ball already gone by. He chuckled at the stunned expression on Dixon's face.

"What the hell setting did you have that on?"

"Oh, around one hundred and fifty miles per hour, along with being a sinker."

Dixon shook his head, then broke out into a wide grin. "With your penchant for pranks, I'm not sure you're the best one to be running that machine."

"Now. Now. Where's your sense of adventure?" Tucker teased.

Dixon's gaze flared with sensual heat. "I'm up for anything you are."

For the first time since that night, Tucker didn't get antsy with the obvious double entendre. Instead, he accepted the small challenge in the spirit it had been offered. The game and friendship came first. Once he improved enough to seize his starting position back, he'd look ahead.

He inclined his head toward Dixon. "Remember that."

"I plan on it." Dixon gave him a small salute, picked up the bat, and took up his batter's stance. "Ready."

Tucker changed the settings back to a more realistic selection and hit the Start button.

Dixon swung and hit the ball square, sending it flying powerfully to the back of the cage.

Thirty minutes later, they entered the visitor's locker room to change into their uniform for the game. As it was still fairly early, none of the rest of the guys had arrived yet. The team's uniform manager had, though.

Every locker sported a freshly cleaned and pressed uniform on a hanger. The white background made the large black numbers on the back of the jerseys stand out. Naturally, Tucker gravitated to his shirt. On the bench in front of him a couple of rolls of black tape waited for someone to utilize them. Some of the players thought the tape helped with blood flow and muscle healing. Tucker didn't argue but also didn't really agree. In his opinion, a shifter just needed to change forms to heal. That's how it normally worked, except in cases with more severe injuries. The aches and pains from being an athlete were commonplace and nothing to really pay too much attention to. Yet, if the players thought the tape gave them an extra boost, then so be it.

He glanced up at the shirts, then back down at the tape. An idea began to take shape.

"Uh-oh." Dixon's voice curried his attention.

"What?" Tucker turned to face him.

"I've seen that look before. You've got trouble on the mind." Dixon opened his locker door.

"Trouble? Me?" Tucker grinned. "Well… maybe a bit of play anyway."

Dixon arched an eyebrow. "Care to fill me in?"

"I was just thinking that perhaps these jerseys need a number alternation."

Dixon looked at the tape. "How so?"

"It's wide enough. We can just add a number here and there." Tucker picked up the roll and pulled off a large piece.

"Scissors and paper." Dixon hurried around the corner before coming back with a short pair, presumably from the equipment manager's toolbox he brought along on each away game. "Let's use the number one on your jersey as an outline." He folded the paper and made marks to resemble the official number. "We can use this for a guide. Cut the tape to match the outline of the numbers." Once done, he handed the scissors to Tucker. "I'll let you do the honors."

"You know they will just pull the tape right off."

"Good point." Tucker considered the situation. "Super glue." Dixon helped him pilfer around until they found a tube in the equipment room.

Tucker went to work cutting out a couple of dozen. As he finished, he handed the artwork to Dixon, who stuck the number on the back of a jersey. The number six became sixty-one. Nine became nineteen. And, Tucker's personal favorite, ninety-one became 911.

Dixon took a moment to stare at the sixty-one shirt. "I wonder." He collected some more tape, cute a couple of smaller pieces, then attached them to the garment. "There."

Tucker laughed. "Sixty-nine, huh?"

"Yep." Dixon grinned proudly.

"You do know that Trigger will be fit to be tied."

"Bring it on." Dixon's eyes shone with mischief.

Tucker found the brilliance compelling. He'd never paid much attention before, but Dixon seemed to be one of the more serious players. Now that he had inside knowledge of what the game meant to his friend, Tucker finally understood. While he needed to get his head back in the game and step up his play, Dixon needed to rediscover fun. Together, they could possibly reach both goals.

Dixon attached the last bit of tape with an amused grin.

"I can't wait to see their faces."

Dixon matched his smile. "Oh, yeah. This is going to be good."

They shared a look, one which made Tucker's breath catch. Not just co-conspirators or partners in crime, but something stronger.

Tucker finally looked away. "We should probably get a bite to eat before time to show up for pregame." His stomach agreed with a hungry rumble.

"Yeah, we should." Dixon closed his locker and returned the scissors on the way out. "What sounds good?"

"Something light. Maybe a sandwich or two. And, nuts to snack on during the game." Some players chewed gum. Others ate sunflower seeds. Tucker preferred nuts. Any kind would work as long as they were slightly salted and of high quality.

"You and your nuts."

Tucker found the comment humorous. "They're quite tasty, you know." He waggled his eyebrows for emphasis.

Dixon groaned loudly. "Bad. Very bad."

"That's me. Bad to the bone." Tucker laughed. They stepped out of the facility and into the late morning air. "Remind me to visit a shop or two when we have some downtime."

"Okay. What do you need?"

"Props."

Dixon blinked, but Tucker only smiled. One part of his game was back up to par. He hoped the rest would soon follow. Until then, he could lighten things up a little in the locker rom. After all, what fun was hanging out with a bunch of guys if you couldn't get their goat now and again?

"WHAT THE hell happened to my number?" Graham turned his shirt this way and that.

The rest of the guys murmured in astonishment and irritation at the addition to their game shirts.

"You think yours is bad. Look at mine." Trigger thrust his jersey toward Graham.

"Sixty-nine." Graham burst out laughing. "Is that a suggestion?"

Trigger's face morphed from annoyance to hot sexual desire in the blink of an eye.

Graham stepped closer and brushed his lips over Trigger's. "Later, mate. After the game."

Trigger groaned softly, kissed Graham with brief intensity, then put some space between them. The love and heated sparks between the two men couldn't be missed.

"Anyone else scent the lust in the air?" Mack asked.

"I thought that was pheromones?" Dixon replied.

Trigger rolled his eyes. "Juvenile. All of you." He raked the room with a stern glare.

Tucker strolled around the corner. "What's this about Trigger all hot and bothered? Again? Didn't we just go through this mating season crap not too long ago?"

"Shut it, puppy." Trigger added a menacing growl for effect.

"Why do I have 911 on my jersey? Does that mean I'm the person to rescue the rest of the team in the case of a horrible outing?" Wiley frowned at his shirt, still hanging up in front of his locker. He tugged at the tape to no avail. It didn't budge.

"If we have to rely on you to save our asses, we're in deep shit," Trigger answered with a smirk.

Wiley flipped him off. "Bite me, grizzly."

"I believe that's my job," Ram insisted.

Wiley grinned wickedly. "True."

All the playfulness with the mated pairs sent a wave of jealousy through Dixon. He wanted the same happiness, the gentle teasing, the molten looks that guaranteed a night of decadent sex after the game. All of that and more. With Tucker.

His gaze latched onto the man in question across the room, smiling proudly at what he'd done. *He sure likes to stir up trouble.* Dixon found it amusing and endearing. A sense of humor went a long way in a relationship. Not that he'd had many serious ones. Most of his partners were impulsive one-night stands. A release of tension and an escape. Nothing more. While he wasn't necessarily proud of his fly-by-night experiences, he also knew he was human. Well partly. But the blame lay with his animal side. The need for sexcapades originated from his inner fox most of the time. After all, beastly lust couldn't be denied.

His inner fox agreed when it came to Tucker.

Dixon quickly slipped into his uniform, grinning at the additional number on his back that changed his normal ten to one hundred and one. The game had always been serious for him. Sure, he'd chuckle at the antics of team clowns, but really didn't get too involved. To him, baseball was a business. One he took great care to mold and protect. After all, he had a family name to live up to.

However, this sillier side appealed just as much as the realities of the sport. Probably more so at this moment in his life. He'd enjoyed letting loose and just being an overgrown kid again. Even better, the other players didn't seem to look his direction when it came to blame. Which made the prank that much funnier. Tucker might catch some flak for it, but Dixon most likely would emerge free and clear.

The grumblings echoed through the locker room, but game time waited for no one.

Dixon hurried to the dugout along with the rest of the team.

Banner posted the batting order on the wall, then turned to face the guys. "Tucker, you're designated hitter today. Take advantage of it."

"Yes, sir." Tucker grinned with more confidence than Dixon had seen since Tucker had been demoted to second string.

Dixon glanced at the paper, finding his name on the top of the list. Nothing unusual as he either led off or hit third. Banner hadn't changed things up in two years where Dixon was concerned.

Dixon picked out his bat and prepared for his first chance against Stu. He'd faced the pitcher enough times to know the guy's in, outs, and tricks.

"Batter up!" The umpire took his place behind the catcher at home plate.

Dixon walked to the left side of the batter's box, took a couple of practice swings, then settled in for his turn.

The first ball whizzed by.

"Strike one."

Well, hell. Stu had picked up some power during the off-season. Dixon filed that for future reference. He lifted his back shoulder a notch to offset his natural tendency to let it drop, then lifted his front foot a bit in anticipation of the throw. His timing mechanism worked as he made contact with the next pitch, sending a laser down the third base line, just out of reach of the opponent, and into the far corner.

Dixon put on the jets, rounded first, and made a dash for second. For a second he'd considered trying for third, but Banner's hands-up stop sign made him slow down and jog into second without even a throw to make the race close. Settled safely, he turned his attention back to home plate.

Tucker strode up to the batter's box, chose the right side, and took up his stance. Tucker was a switch hitter and could smack the ball from either side of the plate. A hard-earned talent and one that benefitted the team when it came to pitchers. With his position, he could either pull the ball to right field or hit square down the middle. If his timing was a smidgen early, he'd blast one toward left.

Dixon moved a couple of paces off the bag, his gaze on the signs the catcher flashed the pitcher. While Dixon didn't know their code, he could pick up on a few things now and again. Stu gathered the ball in his glove, glanced back at Dixon, then flung the first pitch.

"Strike one."

Tucker backed out of the box for a second, looked around, then re-entered. He lifted the bat off his shoulder and focused on the pitcher.

Patience, Tucker. Just make contact. The basics.

Dixon willed Tucker to remember the extra batting practice they had that morning. The lessons revisited in preparation for this moment.

The next throw landed in the dirt. The catcher blocked it, gathered it up, then handed it to the umpire for a replacement. Scuffed balls were rejected by pitchers more times than not.

Dixon stepped back on second base, then took a good lead once more.

Stu fired again.

Crack.

"Foul ball." The umpire held up his hands as the ball landed well out of play in the stands.

Dixon turned and trotted back to his original place. "That's it, Tucker." He clapped a couple of times, then bent his knees and lowered his center of gravity a bit in preparation of either running or having to dive back to the base if the catcher caught him trying to steal.

The pitch came. Tucker swung. Another foul ball, this one over the dugout and into the seats.

"Keep it up," Dixon called as he walked back to the base, stepped on the bag, then drifted off a few feet.

Stu twisted to look at Dixon, turned forward, then threw.

The ball exploded off Tucker's bat.

Dixon took a split second to see the ball heading for the far wall. He waited just a beat, until the ball bounced off the top of the center field fence. A ground rule double. Dixon cheered Tucker's success as he rounded third and made his way home.

He returned to the dugout, receiving high fives from fellow teammates. As much as he appreciated their congratulations, he was more pleased with Tucker. The guy listened and their session, so far, seemed to pay off. He made a mental note to repeat the preparation before the next game, giving Tucker a heads-up on the starting pitcher and seeing a few pitches like the opponent favored to toss.

"You make one hell of a batting coach," Banner said.

Dixon shrugged. "It's only one at bat. We'll see as the game goes." Praise, while possibly deserved, never really sat well with him. He always felt like there was room for improvement. *Oh, shit. I sound just like my father.*

"You're selling yourself short." Banner patted him on the back. "Thanks for going out of your way to help Tucker. Not everyone would."

Dixon nodded, stepped around his manager, and sought an empty spot on the bench. He grabbed a bottle of water along the way, opened the lid, and took a long drink. Idly, he watched the next batter walk to the plate, then centered his attention on Tucker.

The guy had been put together right. The strength came through loud and clear despite the uniform covering all those toned muscles.

Tall and strong, he could run with the best while holding his own at second base as an opponent slid into him in an effort to disrupt a double play.

The light breeze caused some movement that caught Dixon's eye. A couple of dark curls had escaped the helmet, tickling at Tucker's nape. Dixon recalled those same curls as he peered down at Tucker, sucking his cock. Unable to resist, he'd run his hand through the silky soft locks and used the hold to encourage Tucker further.

He had to bite back a low moan at the images flashing through his mind and fought a losing battle against his quickly growing erection. At least the discomfort of having a hard-on while wearing a cup put a rapid dent into his sexual fantasies.

"Hey, Dixon. Earth to Dixon."

Hearing his name, Dixon glanced up to find the source of his erotic daydream standing right in front of him.

"You must be deep in thought about something."

You could say that. He sat up straighter and tilted his head. "Sorry, what did you say?"

Tucker grinned widely. "I said your lessons paid off. Thanks."

"You're welcome," Dixon answered automatically.

"I owe you lunch." Tucker nodded and walked over to the cooler. Dixon watched him go with a mixture of pride and want.

He didn't have long to daydream as the next three batters flied out.

"Okay, guys. Let's get out there and show them how it's done." Slade, who drew the starting pitching role for the day, led the way to the field.

Dixon grabbed his glove and followed, pausing only long enough to give Tucker a reassuring pat on the shoulder. "Enjoy the break. You'll be out there in the sweltering heat with the rest of us soon enough."

Tucker snorted, but Dixon caught the hint of brightness in his eyes. Tucker, while far from fully back, had taken the first step. He'd started to believe in himself again.

The rest would come. If Dixon had anything to do with it.

Chapter 9

TUCKER SAT down on the edge of his bed and stared at the television. He flicked through the channels, finding nothing of interest, then punched it back off.

The game had been a decent one with the Predators pulling off a win. He'd ridden the bench, but went three for four, with a double, two singles, and two runs batted in. Not a bad outing at all and a nice start to getting back into Banner's good graces. He had Dixon to thank for that. His instructions and the insight into the starting pitcher were priceless when it came game time. So was the practice in the batting cage. Even the batting coach couldn't hold a candle to what Dixon did for him. Dixon had a calming, uplifting manner about him. No judging, no harshness, simply upbeat and encouraging. Just what Tucker needed right now.

And the view Dixon presented wasn't bad either.

He groaned as the same old issue came around again in a timely fashion. *Just like reflux.* He grinned at the analogy.

The clock caught his attention. Ten p.m. He had time to venture out into the city, but not the desire. Sleep didn't appeal either as he was still wound from the game. Since nothing on television interested him, he found himself at loose ends.

The black duffel bag caught his attention. He got up, dug out the laptop, and fired it up. He tired of solitaire after playing only a couple of games. With nothing much else to do, he went online, read the latest sports news, then found himself doing a search for bisexuality.

He'd heard the term, certainly. Understood the basics, but couldn't quite put his finger on the fact that he'd always thought himself straight until one life-changing night.

Information appeared in the form of dozens of links to sites. He chose the first one, a seemingly reputable site, and started reading.

How long he pored through pages and how many websites he visited, he couldn't say. But, he did have a new understanding of what being bisexual meant and a possible reason he'd just learned that group included him.

He thought about his pack. Since he'd never visited or met them for fear of being torn apart for his mixed genetics, he couldn't say what sexual orientations existed or how a nonstraight person was treated. Considering how they saw nonpurebreds, he didn't have much faith they'd accept any differences, no matter what. Their beliefs really didn't matter, anyway. Not like he'd make a surprise visit any time soon and announce his newfound sexual interests.

He snorted at the ridiculous thought. His whole life had been a study in keeping away and remaining alive. No reason to buck the system now.

Besides, all that truly mattered were the people he counted as friends and teammates. He knew for a fact they embraced everyone, regardless of their sexual orientation or private practices. He'd seen the truth with his own eyes, especially with the two mated gay couples who were part of the team. They were treated just like everyone else. Accepted as family.

What would it be like to be one of those mated couples? To spend the days and nights with the one you loved above all others? To have that special person in the world who could respect and love you for who you were?

He felt a pang of longing. After years of being a playboy, he'd grown up. Saw something besides cheap dates and fast women. He'd changed his tune completely.

Boy howdy, have I changed my tune.

If only he could navigate a path through this perplexing monkey wrench thrown into the cogs of his life. Scientific data was one thing. Firsthand experience and advice was another.

Ram. He was bi. Maybe he could shine some light on things.

Tucker checked the clock again, crossed his fingers that it wasn't too late, or he'd be interrupting anything, stepped out into the hallway, and to the hotel room that Wiley and Ram shared. He stuck his ear to the wood, heard nothing to indicate they were busily engaged in sex, and blew out a sigh of relief. A little more confident, he rapped on the door.

Wiley answered. "Tucker. Is something wrong?"

"No. I was just wondering if I could talk to Ram."

"Sure." Wiley held the door open, then closed it behind him.

Ram sat on the couch next to the balcony doors. "What's up?"

A bit of nerves ramped up. Tucker took a deep breath and forced himself to follow through with what he'd come to do. "I was wondering if I could ask you some questions."

"Okay."

"About being bi." Tucker said the words in a rush.

"Of course. Have a seat." Ram gestured to one of the plush chairs nearby.

Tucker looked at Wiley with uncertainty. He didn't want to cause any strife between mates, and what Ram said might rub Wiley the wrong way. "Maybe this isn't a good time…."

Wiley grasped Tucker's shoulder. "I don't have any secrets from my mate. And, he doesn't from me. So, whatever you need to know, just ask. It won't bother me at all."

Tucker recognized the truth in Wiley's face and heard it in his voice. He glanced over to Ram and saw the same reflected on Ram's face. He gave a quick nod and sat down.

Wiley positioned himself next to Ram, then linked their hands together.

"What do you want to know?"

It's game time. Tucker hadn't really made a mental list of questions. He'd just reacted with gut impulse. Now, he tried to formulate his many questions into logical sentences. He started with the basics, hoping to springboard from there.

"I've been doing some online research. Read some information, scientific data and then some. That doesn't really help explain why me. Why now? Why with…?"

"Dixon?" Ram asked.

"Yeah."

"I take it you didn't have a clue you liked men until you hooked up with Dixon?"

"No."

"Never checked out another guy's ass? Looked at his smile? Thought he was hot as hell?" Ram tossed out.

"Nope." Tucker thought back. "Not that I can ever recall. Guys were friends. Teammates. Acquaintances. Even rivals for the same girl. Yeah, I noticed if they were in shape or the clothes they wore or car they drove. That kind of stuff. But nothing that made me sit up and pant like a dog in heat."

Wiley chuckled.

Ram smiled with amusement. "It happens like that sometimes."

"Like what?" Tucker sat forward and folded his hands together.

"That just any man won't do. You're bi deep down, but only one man will bring that side out and into the open." Ram scratched his chin.

"I'm still struggling with that," Tucker admitted.

"Listen. Trying to deny being bisexual is like trying to reject the animal part of you. As kids we had to go through all those growing pains with learning how to work with our inner beast instead of against him. Two halves of the same whole. You can't have one without the other. It's just who you are," Ram advised. "There are rewards for accepting who you are. You already have them with being a shifter. You'll find more when you accept being bisexual."

"I'm getting there." Tucker knew Ram spoke the truth. The facts didn't lie. Unfortunately, his mind seemingly could lust after Dixon even though he still couldn't quite label and organize this new development in the same head. He forced himself back on topic. "So, you're saying that Dixon is that guy?"

"Ever heard of 'gay for you'?" Wiley asked.

"Nope."

Wiley blinked. "Where have you been, buddy?"

"Working my ass off on the baseball diamond? And chasing girls in between." Tucker didn't realize he'd spoken the last part out loud until Ram responded.

"You did that, all right. Never enough women to satisfy you." Ram tilted his head and appraised Tucker for a long moment. "Ever wonder why you never settled down with them? Or married one of them?"

Tucker dropped his gaze to the carpet. "I never wanted commitment. They wanted me to scratch their itch. I wanted the same.

That's the way it was." He peered up at Ram. "You think there's more to it than that?"

Ram shrugged. "Could be."

"That maybe I didn't want to settle down with them because they were just not the one, they weren't even of the correct sex?" The idea took hold.

"I'd still say Dixon is the key. You just said you'd never looked at another man until him." Wiley stretched his long legs in front of him.

"Right," Ram answered. "I think we're back to the 'gay for you' idea."

Tucker caught their drift. "You think that I'm not happy with women, but never looked at men until Dixon. I might never want another man either."

"Bingo. Something is special about Dixon. He's the only man you wanted. Still want, if I'm not mistaken," Wiley said.

Tucker didn't bother to answer. With everything being so up in the air, he hadn't really sat down and explored his feelings for Dixon. Until he could accept that he wanted to be with another man, nothing else really could be ironed out.

"You were with a woman the other night, though." Ram stared at him. "How was that?"

A bit uncomfortable, Tucker squirmed in his seat. "It wasn't the best." Hell, it ranked as one of the worst sexual experiences he'd ever had. The woman was hot, sexy, and more than willing to do anything he wanted as long as she got her rocks off. He'd had high hopes, only for them to be dashed from the start. He ended up distracted with flashes of his time with Dixon popping in at the most inconvenient times.

"Couldn't get Dixon out of your mind?" Wiley asked.

Tucker's gaze flew to him. "How?"

Wiley grinned. "Ram and I didn't have smooth sailing right after we were together the first time." He looked over at Ram.

"I had some issues accepting things." Ram lifted their joined hands and kissed Wiley's. "In all honesty, even if I had taken a woman to bed, I believe I would have had the same situation as you did, Tucker. I couldn't forget how great the sex was with Wiley and that would ruin me for anyone else."

Tucker processed their comments. *Maybe Dixon did ruin me for anyone else.* The sex had been hotter than anything he'd yet experienced. Decadent. Exciting. Sinful.

So fucking addictive too, his inner wild dog added. *We need him. Want him. He's ours.* A snap of teeth followed, declaring the remarks to be less of a suggestion and more of a strong order.

Tucker ignored the voice, still feeling too off-balanced to deal with two conversations at the same time. Tucker scrubbed his face. "Do you miss being with women?"

Ram shook his head. "Not in the least. I have Wiley and he makes all my dreams come true."

The sincerity in Ram's voice carried easily to Tucker's ears.

"What am I going to do?" The question slipped out unbidden.

"Take some time, figure out what you really want, and then go for it," Wiley advised.

Ram caught Tucker's attention. "You have to be willing to look past what happened and realize the cost or benefit of leaving that event totally in your past, never to be experienced again in your future." He paused a couple of beats. "If it's worth having, it's worth fighting for."

The words soaked in.

He'd found some answers and been left with the biggest question of all. *Can I get over this hurdle, accept this enigma in life, and fight for Dixon?*

No internal response came, not even from his inner beast.

Chapter 10

TUCKER DOVE to the side, catching the ball about a foot in the air right before it hit the earth, smacking his chest and hips into the unforgiving ground. He made sure to keep his glove closed and the ball secure as he pushed up from the ground. After checking the runner stationed at second base, he tossed the ball back to Graham, the pitcher, and dusted himself off.

"Nice grab."

Tucker grinned over at Dixon. "Thanks."

"Always a nose for the ball. Must be a canine thing," Wiley added, tongue-in-cheek. Since all three of them fit into that category, he could get away with the tease.

"Smart-ass," Tucker replied without a hint of anger. In fact, he grinned the whole time.

The improved mood was obvious on Tucker's face, and Dixon felt a combination of relief and happiness. He'd worried that getting benched might make a permanent dent in Tucker's psyche, but that didn't seem to be the case, at least for today. Ever since Banner gave Lance the day off and put Tucker back in his old spot, Tucker seemed to have a bounce in his step. A nice change, if only it would last.

Dixon had been around the game long enough to know that Banner swapped the two men to give Tucker an opportunity to earn his position back. That decision could last one day or a month. No telling what the old manager had up his sleeve. Until then, he crossed his fingers Tucker could put on an impressive show.

Their opponent, the Bay City Bengals, were in the middle of the standings in the infancy of the baseball season. The Predators, on the other hand, had huge expectations after taking the final series to win the championship last season. Each game counted, no matter how talented or challenging the other team. Dixon understood the dynamics well. Not like he could forget with his father coaching over the phone. He'd heard more than an earful this morning about the value of momentum and keeping his average up. Facts he already knew and had taken to heart years ago. Irritated, he'd finally gotten upset enough and hung up. After all, he had enough coaching on the diamond without his perfectionist father joining in.

The crack of a bat pulled him back to the present. A ball bounced once on the packed ground. Tucker backhanded the ball, spun, and threw a missile to Dixon.

Dixon positioned himself between the runner and his base, caught the ball, and lowered his glove for the tag. The runner slid feetfirst right into Dixon.

"Out!"

He heard the word but couldn't focus on anything but his left ankle. After crumpling to the ground, he reached down to hold the area, which throbbed like someone had taken a jackhammer to it. He'd been spiked before, but nothing like this.

Wiley squatted down. "You okay?"

Dixon gritted his teeth. "Yeah. Just give me a hand." He reached out, but no one did the same.

Tucker joined the party. "I think you should stay put. The doc is on his way."

Sure enough, Dr. Monroe, the team physician hurried over. He pushed through the circle of players and kneeled. "Where does it hurt?"

"Ankle." Dixon bit back a growl and a cuss when Dr. Monroe removed his shoe and started to gently rotate the foot around.

"Hmmm." He prodded up the lower leg and back down again. "Definitely need an X-ray."

"It's fine. I can play if someone will just help me up," Dixon snapped. "Hell, one shift and I'll be good as new."

Banner shook his head. "Not happening, kid. So, just do as the doctor orders." He looked at the other players standing around. "If a couple of you guys can manage to get Dixon to the bench, we can continue on with the game."

Tucker took one side and Wiley the other. Together, they supported Dixon as he hopped on one leg all the way through the locker area, then to the medical room right next door. He sat down on the table and snarled at his rotten luck.

"That bastard…."

"I'm sure it wasn't intentional, Dixon." Wiley patted him on the shoulder. "It was a clean slide, just bad luck."

Tucker nodded. "Don't worry. Doc will get you fixed up good as new." He grinned encouragingly. "We have some private lessons planned that I wouldn't miss for the world."

Dixon blew out a breath, his temper cooling at their words. Tucker's comment perplexed him as he searched for a possible double meaning. Knowing he'd never find out the truth at the moment, he filed the question away for later.

"It's fine. Just one quick shift and I'll be back good as new."

"Go on so I can check him out." The doctor shooed the other guys out, leaving him alone with Dixon. The short injury time out wouldn't allow them to stand around, anyway. "Scoot around. I need to take that sock off." He dropped the shoe he'd removed on the field and carried inside to the floor.

Though he was off the ankle, Dixon still cussed a blue streak as stabbing pain once more struck him.

"The spikes broke the skin," Dr. Monroe whispered, probably talking to himself.

Dixon heard him well enough. "That's not the first time or the last time. All part of the game."

Dr. Monroe met his gaze. "Makes this more complicated if that ankle is broken like I think it is."

Dixon swallowed. "Meaning?"

"Meaning an open fracture is a big infection potential. Get bacteria to the bone and it's a huge problem. Cleanliness is paramount at this stage." He sprayed some cool cleaning agent on Dixon's lower leg and foot, then proceeded to scrub lightly with a cloth he'd pulled out of a side cabinet.

Though the doctor was gentle, pain shot up Dixon's leg with every touch. Even he could see the area swelling fast. Dixon bit his lip and remained stoic.

After the soap lathered and no traces of dirt remained, Dr. Monroe placed a towel under Dixon's leg and poured what looked like water from a bottle over it. He repeated the process once more.

The entire time Dixon ran Dr. Monroe's words through his mind. A surge of worry accompanied his thoughts. As a shifter he rarely thought about injuries, even though they were a common part of the game. Shifter genetics allowed them the advantage of healing quickly with a change in forms. He only hoped this would be the case with him.

He closed his eyes, grappled with the discomfort, then reopened them to find a woman positioning a large metal arm over his foot. Dressed in scrubs, she reminded him of a nurse, yet without the stethoscope hanging around her neck. Presumably the X-ray technician Dr. Monroe promised.

She shot him a small smile. "We're going to get a couple of pictures."

"Okay."

She stepped to one wall, picked up a large hunk of material, then draped it over his body from shoulders to knees.

The weight of it surprised him. Before he could even ask, she scurried several feet away, taking the team doctor with her. A beep followed.

After changing his position, she repeated the process, then moved over to allow Dr. Monroe to see the results.

He gave a quick nod. "Just as I thought. That fibula is fractured. Nondisplaced, though. That's good."

Dixon sighed. "No problem. I'll just shift."

"That will help, but first I'm going to have to give you antibiotics to curb any infection that might want to set in. The last thing we want to have to do is deal with osteomyelitis."

The unfamiliar word caused Dixon to blink. "Osteo... what?"

"A bone infection." Dr. Monroe opened the top drawer of what resembled a large tool chest. He pulled out a glass bottle filled with white liquid and a syringe. "A shot daily for two or three days. Once the wound is closed, the chances decrease immensely."

Dixon watched him carefully, noted the size of the needle, and grimaced. "And where are you going to stick that?"

Dr. Monroe grinned. "Your butt, where else?"

"That's what I was afraid of." Dixon felt like a five-year-old getting his immunizations.

He scooted around, lowered his weight to his good leg, then started unbuckling his belt. The sooner they finished, the better.

"I'm going to put you in a walking boot too. And give you a few pain pills. That will take pressure off the fracture and protect those spike wounds. You'll just need to take it off at night when you're in bed."

"Okay." Dixon went ahead and shucked his shirt as well. Task complete, he sat back down to take off his other shoe and sock, fully remove his pants and underwear, and place everything next to him. Better to keep his uniform off the floor since he had to put it back on.

"Ready when you are."

Dixon bit back a groan, stood up, and gave the team doctor an easy target. He hissed at the large sting and burn. "Damn. Did you use the needle made for an elephant?"

Dr. Monroe chuckled, finished, and stuck a Band-Aid over the spot. "It's thick stuff. Gotta use a bigger needle to get it in."

"I'll say." Dixon jiggled a little, hoping it would ease the hurt. No such luck. "Can I shift now?"

"Go for it."

Dixon wasted no time, inwardly reached for his animal side, felt the tingle, and turned into his gray fox alter ego.

"Cute."

Dixon glared up at the team doctor and snorted. He would have growled but figured since he needed more shots, pissing off the guy giving them would be a really bad idea. Dr. Monroe might actually dig out the elephant-sized needles just for spite. Instead, he gingerly walked around, trying out the leg. While a bit tender, it seemed to hold up well enough. He made a circle around the room, then returned to the table. In a flash, he morphed back into his human form.

He grabbed his clothes and started pulling them back on, making sure to leave the shoe off his injured foot.

"Here." Dr. Monroe handed over a bottle of pills and a glass of water. "Anti-inflammatory. It'll help with swelling and pain, but won't make you goofy. Take one twice per day for a couple of days at least."

"Okay." He opened the bottle, took one out, and swallowed it down with the help of the provided drink.

"This is the walking boot I was talking about." Dr. Monroe held it up.

The device looked like a plastic slip-on blue cast. Better than dealing with plaster in the heat, he'd imagine. And the easy removal had its perks.

He finished dressing and sat back on the table, letting his legs swing free.

Dr. Monroe placed the boot on, made a couple of small adjustments, then gestured for him to walk.

Dixon did, finding the task definitely different and noisier than before. Though the plastic didn't weigh much, it sure felt like his foot had gained a good ten pounds. Awkward came to mind. He frowned.

"You'll get used to it. I'm putting you on the injured reserve list for this series. We'll recheck you in a week or so back at home base."

"A week?" Dixon scowled. "That long?"

"Yep."

"I can shift another time or three. That should take care of it."

Dr. Monroe stared at Dixon with a stern expression. "I don't care if you shift fifty times in the next hour, your body still needs some time to strengthen that bone and make sure there's no residual problem. Certainly, you're not playing for a few days, so settle down, quit complaining, and deal."

Dixon blinked at the hard tone. "I'm not worried about playing." The confession slipped out.

"Then what has you in such a hurry?"

"I have obligations." Dixon blew out a breath, glanced toward the door, then back again. "I'm helping Tucker with extra practices. I need to be able to do that."

Dr. Monroe gave a brief nod. "Tell you what. You can give him all the verbal help you want. Throw out pointers, give him the lowdown on teams and pitchers. Be the voice of wisdom for him. But—" He pinned Dixon with his gaze. "Find someone else for him to chase balls with."

Dixon considered the directions. "I can still hit balls to him, right?"

"Yeah. Light stuff. The whole idea is that you don't put any huge force on that ankle for a few days. Tight turns, running full-out, jumping, and landing will stress that area and slow down healing. Not to mention hurt like hell. But, walking and doing some low impact stuff is okay."

Relief washed over Dixon. He smiled for the first time since being carted into the medical room. "Thanks, Doc." He held out his hand.

Dr. Monroe shook it. "Don't do anything stupid."

"No chance." Dixon walked out of the room, still getting the hang of the boot. He headed straight for the dugout and plopped down on the bench. The pain reduced to a dull ache, but one that proved manageable, at least so far.

The Predators were batting, so nearly all the players were there. Each one looked his direction, peered down at the boot, then back to his face. He offered up a small grin. "Just a precaution."

Banner came over. "How long?"

"A week, according to Doc."

"Not bad. Good thing you're a shifter. That injury would put you out for the season, most likely, if you were human."

"One of the benefits of being part canine," Wiley answered.

"With that device, we can hear you coming a mile away," Trigger pointed out.

Tucker shook his head at the grizzly shifter and ambled over. Concern radiated in his eyes. "You okay?"

Dixon nodded. "Yeah. Broken ankle, but a shift pretty much took care of it. Since the spikes broke the skin, I'm on antibiotics for a couple of days." He still felt the small tingle where Dr. Monroe gave him the shot. Resisting the urge to rub it, he chose to ignore it and not dwell on having to endure another one the next day.

"So, you need to rest." Tucker's voice remained unchanged but carried a hint of regret or possibly uncertainty.

Dixon could almost read his mind. "Doc said I could still coach, just not be on the field diving after line drives, or in the batter's box trying to knock one out of the park. Not until we get back home, anyway."

Tucker's shoulders relaxed as did his expression. He sat down next to Dixon. "How about this? You provide the helpful hints and I'll drive you around."

Dixon tapped his injured left leg. "I can still drive. The advantage of having an automatic transmission. Don't need the left foot for much."

"True." Tucker turned his attention back to the field. "How about I let you be my co-conspirator instead?"

Dixon arched an eyebrow. "Like before?"

"Uh-huh."

"You've got a deal."

Despite not being able to play, Dixon felt pretty damn good. He'd still get to share insight and hang out with the team. In addition, he'd partner up with Tucker on his next prank. Not a bad deal after all.

He reclined against the backrest and pondered his situation. Not being out at third base wasn't the end of the world. Heck, he found the reprieve almost nice. No pressure to perform. No imminent phone calls from his father, tearing his style apart, piece by little tiny piece. Instead, he could just enjoy being a player.

Ares stood in the box, facing one of the better pitchers in the league. Miles had a cannon of an arm but also could throw a sneaky off-speed pitch that would catch hitters out of sorts most of the time.

Dixon studied the guy's delivery, then Ares's swing. He chopped at the ball. Once. Twice. Then fanned the plate when Miles took something off and hooked a decent pitch at his knees and to the inside.

Ares trotted down the steps with a scowl on his face. "I can't hit that fucking breaking ball, no matter what I try."

Dixon turned to the rookie with interest. "You can if you catch the little drop of his glove hand and the slight hesitation in his timing."

Ares grumbled under his breath. "His delivery is the damn same as with his fastball. I've watched."

Dixon pursed his lips. "Not quite. I'll let you in on a little observation or two."

Ares lifted his head and stared at Dixon. "You're serious?"

"Yeah. Sit down and we'll analyze some things." He gestured to the empty spot next to him with his head.

Ares did as bidden.

"As you know, most pitchers are creatures of habit. The trick is trying to find very tiny differences in the delivery that will clue you in to what's coming." Dixon gestured toward Miles. "The way he holds his glove. The lift of his leg. The grip on the ball when it leaves his hand."

Together they watched him throw several more balls, Dixon noting subtle changes that seemed to occur with consistency. He pointed out each one.

Lance came over to take a place next to Ares. He leaned over and listened in. A couple more of the older guys did the same.

"How do you know all this?" Tucker asked.

Dixon shrugged. "I was schooled in hitting from day one. It's been drilled into me since I could pick up a bat. After all those years, it finally sank in." He smiled softly. While he and his father might not get along, he couldn't deny the results of his father's influence. "I also watch a lot of videos. To know the pitcher is to find his weaknesses."

"You live and breathe the game," Lance said.

Dixon mentally cringed. *He's right. I have no fucking life.* Instead of lamenting his lot, he focused on helping out where he could. "I spend a lot of time trying to improve, yeah. But, nothing worthwhile is easy. All the talent in the world can't make up for doing your homework."

The guys nodded in acknowledgment.

Oddly enough, Dixon discovered something new. Even with a bum foot and benched for the series, he was having a good time. More fun than he'd had while stationed at his normal starting position, that was for sure.

Sharing his knowledge came easy and natural. To have receptive ears all around provided a confidence boost and gave him a sense of importance. He liked coaching. Reveled in it. At last he'd found a niche that offered up great opportunities while giving back.

Something to think about, anyway.

He couldn't play the game forever and he needed a backup plan. Right now, he feared burnout had seized hold, and he no longer saw the stadium as anything but a cubicle where he came to spend his days at work. As long as he played, his father's perfectionist views would always hang over his head with his calls from his father filled with judgment and critiques. The constant, impossible expectations ruined the game for him. But, as a coach, he'd shake free of the overbearing burden and fly free. For the first time in his life.

Hope sparked with the idea.

Tucker stood, walked over to grab his bat, and made his way to the warm-up circle. Dixon watched him every step of the way. The snap of muscles in Tucker's conditioned body couldn't be denied. They drew Dixon's attention and made him recall how glorious Tucker looked naked. As long as he lived, he'd never forget that night. Even if Tucker seemed intent on doing just that.

Tucker took the first pitch, laying off as it went outside. The next came inside. Tucker just managed to stop his swing in time. He reset his stance, then waited.

Miles gathered up his body, then exploded out as he fired.

Tucker swung.

Crack.

The ball shot over the head of the second baseman and into center field.

A nice single.

Tucker stopped at first, stared back at the dugout, and gave a thumbs-up.

The gesture reaffirmed Dixon's contentment for the moment. Helping Tucker to get back on track gave him more happiness and feelings of success than if he stepped up to the plate and hit an out-of-the-park homerun.

That's pretty damn significant.

Dixon knew he was looking at his potential future. But, with that came a big splash of reality.

Coaches were traded more than players in the league. A bad season, new management, even disagreement with a top-level athlete was enough to can a coach. While he might enjoy teaching the other players, especially the up-and-coming ones, he saw reality. No one started out in the majors for their very first coaching position. They did their time in the minors or at the college level and worked their way up. That took years with still no guarantee of making it to the top.

In order to change his career to a new direction, Dixon had to pack up his bags and leave Preston.

And Tucker as well.

The thought sent a pang straight to his heart.

Chapter 11

"WHAT ARE we looking for exactly?" Dixon asked. He still wore the boot on his left leg, but it didn't slow him down in the least. The click, though, allowed Tucker to easily keep track of his buddy especially when walking on cement floors.

"I'm not sure, but I'll know it when I see it," Tucker replied as he scanned the shelves.

They'd finished the series in Florida and arrived home last night. Tucker's batting average went up dramatically with the help of Dixon's coaching every day before the game, along with some extra time in the batting cages. Banner even let Tucker play second base each game after Dixon's injury as Lance had been moved over to cover third. No errors to report. And a pretty nice series overall.

He'd mentioned his agenda today to Dixon, who volunteered to tag along "to learn the art of pranking from the best." Tucker didn't mind. Besides, he'd promised. A favor for a favor.

They'd fallen into a companionable friendship and worked well together over the past week. The mornings they spent in an extra baseball practice with just the two of them or perhaps an assistant coach or two to help out, especially on fielding skills. Afterward, they had downtime before either afternoon practice or pregame. If they had a late game, then they'd sleep in and hit the field earlier than the other guys in order to get some extra work in.

The effort had paid off.

While he wasn't back on the starting roster, he made the best of his opportunity. And, intended to do so every time he took the field.

In the meantime, he had some vague ideas on how to keep the guys loose before the game. They involved a couple of stops and some odd purchases.

He turned down another aisle of the toy store and heard Dixon clicking along behind him, slowly, as if he checked everything out with interest. The thought of Dixon hanging out in a toy store amused Tucker but didn't surprise him. Not now. From what he gathered, Dixon didn't have a great childhood, with his father to blame for pressuring him constantly about baseball. While the sport had been meant for fun, he doubted Dixon saw it that way. More like an endless job while growing up. Just business as usual in his eyes. No wonder he'd always been so serious at the ballpark.

Yet, he'd seen another side of Dixon recently. The coach. The unselfishness and caring, the dedication and pride. He might not be able to get on the field with his injury, but he helped in other ways. Not only the team, but individual players who took the time to listen.

Not every man would give up his hard-earned knowledge. Dixon did gladly.

Tucker thought he'd come to know Dixon over the last year or so. But, he saw the baseball player, not really much deeper. The last couple of weeks had shown him the true man. One whose smile made his heart kick and his insides melt like ice cream on a hot summer's day. One whose body jolted his desires into high gear. One whose sweet nature touched him deeper than all the rest.

Dixon was the whole package. A precious gift he'd lose if he didn't face the facts and stand up like a man.

I want him.

He glanced back at Dixon, found him looking over a sea of toys, before bending to read the writing on a box. Tucker's breath caught at the sight of Dixon's rear pointed in his direction. His mind might still be processing the changes, but his body only knew one thing. Dixon made him hungry, hot, and turned on.

Dixon pulled a mechanical dinosaur off the shelf to inspect it further.

Tucker grinned. The guy needed to get in touch with his inner child, and he vowed to make it happen. Starting with incorporating him into the business of pranking the other players.

Pleasing Dixon and making him laugh grew to utmost priority in Tucker's mind. Dixon had given so much of himself, and Tucker intended to pay him back.

I just want to make him happy.

Then tell him how you feel. That you want him. His inner animal cajoled. A nice change from his usual demanding tone.

It's not that easy. You know that.

Nothing ventured, nothing gained.

Yeah, yeah.

Tucker scanned the closest aisle as they ambled around the toy store. The doll department, where they started, hadn't interested him a bit. Even the toys that changed from human to animal didn't quite make the grade. So, they'd continued searching.

A shape to his right caught his eye. He strode over, picked up the item, and grinned. "Oh, yeah."

Dixon came over. "A windup rat?"

"Yep. Can you imagine? Just wind it up and let it go in the locker room?" The thought provoked images of players scrambling, hollering, and maybe trying to squash the thing. Tucker wondered who'd scream and run and who'd stand up and fight the little vermin.

Dixon shook his head and grinned. "You're a mess."

"What else is new?" Tucker tucked the rat under his arm and led the way toward the back of the store. He had another plan, which involved sporting equipment.

An hour later, he and Dixon placed four oversized bags of stuff in the back of Dixon's SUV. Tucker shut the hatch and climbed into the passenger's seat.

"Where now?"

"Drug store."

Dixon blinked. "Do I want to know what you're getting from there?"

"Probably not." Tucker smiled. As a rule, shifters didn't use human medication. Their metabolism was different enough that the drugs didn't act in the same way for their species. Not to mention, a simple shift could heal just about anything.

"Okayyy." Dixon placed the key in the ignition and started the engine.

"It's that or the sex store," Tucker tossed out.

Dixon's lips parted even as his eyebrows furrowed. "Nope. I'm not going to ask." He shook his head and pulled out onto the road. Two blocks away, he turned into the parking lot of a pharmacy.

"I'll just be a second." Tucker jumped out and hurried inside. He found the correct area, spied the big tubes of lube, and collected three of them. On the way out, he found another interesting item. An invisible gel that turned colors when in contact with the skin. He grinned wickedly and added that to his armful of stuff.

The cashier gave him an odd look but didn't say much besides the total amount owed. Tucker gladly paid up, took his bag in hand, and walked out the door and straight to Dixon's vehicle.

"That's it?" Dixon asked.

"Yep." Tucker pulled out one of the tubes.

"Holy shit." Dixon gaped at the extra-large container of lube. "I'm afraid to ask what you intend to do with that."

Tucker grinned. "I did get two others just like it."

"Plan on having an orgy?"

"Well...."

"Really?" Curious interest along with a healthy dose of shock covered Dixon's face.

Tucker laughed. "Actually, I thought about coating the bases with it."

For a second Dixon didn't do anything more than sit in his seat and stare at Tucker. Slowly, an evil grin creased his face. "So when they slide in, they'll keep right on going."

"Exactly."

"Got to give you credit for imagination." Dixon started up the SUV once again. "Still need the sex store?"

Tucker blew out a breath. "No, not now." He'd visited the place more than once, always searching for something new and exciting to spice up his sex life. That didn't embarrass him in the least. However, the thought of taking Dixon with him made him edgy and uncertain.

"Are we ever going to talk about what happened?" Dixon asked.

"I'm...." Tucker bit his lip. He couldn't get the night out of his mind or quit checking Dixon out. That was personal. Actually discussing the event with Dixon went deeper. More intimate. And not without a large amount of trepidation.

Denial gets you nowhere. Grow a pair and buck up. His inner wild dog yapped at him again.

It's not time.

A piss-poor excuse and you know it. The beast growled at him. *Take him home and play hide the sausage already.*

Tucker frowned with irritation. *Knock it off. I'll know when the time is right.*

Uh-huh. Just take some of that lube for yourself. You'll be spending so much time jacking off that you'll chafe.

Enough. Tucker snapped his teeth together.

"Problem?" Dixon asked.

"No."

Dixon eyed him for a long moment before driving out onto the road. "Ready for lunch? My treat."

For a second, Tucker considered backing out. He glanced over at Dixon and decided to follow through with their original plans. His professional life had started looking up since Dixon stepped into the picture and he'd been having fun as well. Not ready for the good times to stop, he stepped up to the figurative plate.

"I thought I was paying since you've been spending all the time on private lessons."

He could show us some more private lessons.

Shut up.

Tucker ignored the voice in his head and peered out the front windshield.

"If you're sure." Dixon stopped for a stoplight.

"Yep. Your choice. Where do you want to go?"

"I thought pizza."

"I happen to like that too."

Tucker smiled, relieved to be over that small bump in the road today. Casual teammates and friends he could do well. A bi lover was a lot harder to wrap his mind around. He was trying. That's all he could really say.

Well, that and he felt more attraction for Dixon than he had for any of the women he'd been with lately. Including Gloria. Before, they were trophy girlfriends, a status in his life. A reminder of how far he'd come.

I was so fucking shallow.

He grimaced at how superficial he'd been. Though, the women were of the same mentality. All wanted a notch on their bedpost as much as he did. Some pursued higher ambitions by trying to get a ring on their finger, but he called their game and walked away.

Now, he saw relationships a bit differently. Thanks to the guys on the team and spending some quality time with one gray fox shifter. With Dixon, it wasn't about prestige or money. It revolved around feelings.

Something he wasn't so adept at dealing with.

The shock of his newly discovered bisexual status still rattled him, but less since he'd had time to process and a bit of help from Ram and Wiley. His research reassured him as well. Maybe he was a late bloomer. Maybe he was simply gay only for Dixon. Maybe he'd just buried that part of himself until now.

The facts were, his bi nature wasn't going away. And, to turn away from that part was to reject himself.

As Ram said, it's the same as trying to ignore the beast side. The result would only tear a shifter apart emotionally and psychologically. Just like they'd all had to do from a young age, each shifter both accepted and embraced their animal half. No big deal. The benefits of the combination proved quite rewarding.

The same would happen for acknowledging his bisexual self. At least that's what Ram advised.

Tucker had no reason to doubt him.

Just take the bull by the horns already.

He sucked in air and steeled himself. "I liked what we did."

"You mean changing the numbers on the jerseys?"

Tucker shook his head. "That too, but I was talking about sex. It was… hot. Really great."

Dixon glanced at him. "But?"

"There's no 'but.' I'm bi. I know that now. Still trying to grasp what all that means. Though, I'm no longer running."

Dixon gave a quick nod. "I'm glad."

"I just need time."

After pulling into a parking space, Dixon cut the engine. He swiveled around to meet Tucker's gaze, then trailed a finger over Tucker's cheek. "There's no rush. None at all. I want you; that's a given. But only if you want me too."

The tender caress touched deeper than skin level. He'd never known a simple stroke could be so gentle. Sensual. Wondrous. Tucker swallowed. "I think I do. It's just...." Words failed him.

"A huge change and one that's mind-boggling."

Tucker's mouth fell open. "How?"

"I get it, Tucker. How do you think I felt when I realized I was gay? Went through all kinds of confusion. Questioning. Wondering."

Tucker had never thought of it that way. His nervousness eased a little.

"Everyone I knew was straight. It took a while to realize why I was different. Not wrong, just different from others. I analyzed the shit out of things. Trying to figure out the whys and hows. Finally, I looked around, discovered some facts, found out that I was gay, and figured out a way to accept me for what I am. After working through all the crap, I was a hell of a lot happier."

Tucker soaked in Dixon's words. "What about your parents? Did they understand?" He could only imagine how difficult it would be growing up gay with absolutely no support system in place. Probably the reason some kids decide to run away rather than stay and suffer at the hand of the people that were supposed to love and protect them.

Dixon smiled softly. "My mother didn't care in the least, but she's always been 100 percent behind me in everything." He paused for a second. "That was one thing my father did right, too. He pulled me aside, told me he'd known for a while that I was gay. Said I was still his son no matter if I wanted women, men, or life-sized stuffed toy sheep."

Tucker chucked. "Sheep, huh?"

"Those don't entice me, sorry," Dixon answered with a hint of humor. "But you do."

Tucker's amusement slowly turned serious as he returned to the core of the issue. He had support in his team members. That he knew for a fact. It was the rest of the world, including his mother that concerned him. He shouldn't care, but he did.

Add in the fact that he still wasn't confident enough to dabble with men and he second-guessed his every step. "It gets better?"

Dixon grinned. "Oh, yeah. Just give yourself some slack. Things eventually fall into place."

"Promise?"

"Yep." Dixon leaned in, cupped Tucker's cheek, and very lightly brushed his lips over Tucker's. "That's a promise." He dropped his hand. "Now, let's go eat."

Feeling better, Tucker smiled in return. "Good idea."

TUCKER SAT still as Dixon cut the engine of his SUV after parking in front of Tucker's apartment building. Dinner had been fun, laid-back, and quite enjoyable. He'd gladly do it again, even if he had to foot the bill each time.

"Tonight was fun. Good food. Great company."

Dixon swiveled in his seat and grinned. "Definitely."

They stared at one another for a long moment before Tucker broke eye contact. "I guess I should be going."

"If you have to."

Dixon's low tone made Tucker's stomach flip.

In truth, he didn't want to the night to end. They had the next day off, and he didn't have to be up at the crack of dawn. Not to mention, he intended to use the time for more practice. That involved Dixon, if he didn't mind giving up his day off. He went with his gut.

"You want to come up? The Stars game is probably still on."

Dixon tilted his head. "Just the game, right?"

Too much, too soon. Tucker swallowed. "Yeah."

"That's just fine by me." He paused a second. "Like I said, there's no rush. I'm here when and if you're ready to come to me."

Reassured, Tucker quickly nodded. "One day at a time."

"Yep." Dixon climbed out of the vehicle, opened the hatch, and grabbed a couple of bags. Tucker took the rest. After Dixon secured the car, they walked up to the front door.

Tucker used his key to get in, held the door open for Dixon, then hooked a right. They walked down to the end of the hall together until Tucker stopped, used a different key, and opened the door to his apartment.

"After you." He gestured inside.

Dixon walked forward. Tucker collected his stuff, then followed, automatically shutting and locking the door behind him.

"Nice place."

"Thanks." Tucker glanced around the familiar apartment. It was a temporary home. Easy to care for, especially since he was gone so much during the season. Upscale, the apartment showed off his affluence, filled with brand names and top-of-the-line items. The furniture sported leather while the hardwood floor glistened in a nice contrast of browns. Two bedrooms and ample space for a single guy proved the clincher a while back when he decided to rent the place. Now, it almost appeared cold and empty.

He thought of Dixon's house and a twinge of rightness echoed through his mind.

I'm losing my freaking mind.

He shoved the forlorn internal comments aside and focused on the present. Unloading his goodies, he placed his bags next to the door, then helped Dixon position his right next to them. "Here's good. That way I won't forget them."

Dixon shook his head. "Even when the chips are down, you're always thinking of pranks."

Tucker nodded. "Life is too short to be serious all the time. Besides, it's fun to yank the other guys' chains. Makes all the planning and plotting worth it."

"I guess so." Dixon turned around and headed toward the couch.

"Want a beer?"

"Sure."

Tucker went to the fridge, pulled two out, then returned to find Dixon already sitting on the couch with remote in hand. *Ballsy making himself right at home.* He didn't mind in the least, though, just smiled and handed the beverage over.

"Thanks." Dixon twisted the cap off and took a sip while turning on the TV and flipping through channels until he landed on a baseball game. "You're right. The Stars are still playing."

The Stars were tough opponents that gave them hell each time they played. All the teams were good in the league. The Stars were just a step above the rest.

Tucker settled down at the end of the couch and stretched his feet out in front of him. He flicked his gaze from the game to Dixon and back again. Rarely did he have company over and never to just sit back and watch television. Too mundane an evening. Besides, most of the people who visited were female and he had much more erotic plans for them.

Comfortable and content, Tucker realized that hanging out with Dixon proved to be more fun than he'd thought. Relaxing, even. No pressure to do much more than stare at the screen. Conversation was optional as was anything and everything else.

"Pulaski is hot this year." Dixon gestured toward the game. "He's throwing well, hitting the corners, and has a hell of a lot of movement on the ball."

Tucker smiled to himself. Dixon seemed to always be studying, learning, working hard to get any edge he could. Definitely Mr. Serious and all business when it came to baseball. The trick became how to get him to just let go and enjoy.

"He'll be a challenge to hit."

"Definitely." Dixon took another drink. "When we get close to that series, I'll have to watch a lot of him."

Tucker found the thought of Dixon sitting at home alone, spending hours watching pitchers, to be pretty sad. Sure, to be a good hitter, a guy had to know a pitcher's habits and abilities. A basic part of the game. The part about Dixon doing all that by himself was what tugged at Tucker's heartstrings.

The sacrifices Dixon made for the game and for his teammates began to add up in Tucker's mind. He couldn't say he'd do the same. The fact both shamed him and made Dixon shine more in his eyes.

"Selfish."

"What are you talking about?" Dixon asked.

Tucker grimaced not realizing he spoke the word aloud. "I was just thinking that I've been obsessed with getting to the big leagues all my life. Then, once I got here, figuring that I'd earned my way and that was that.

That somehow just getting there and becoming a starter should ensure that I had the position as long as I wanted it." He ran a hand through his hair and turned to meet Dixon's gaze. "I deserved the demotion. I've been slacking, spending more time goofing off than focusing on my game. You, on the other hand, still work your tail off every day to get better and help all the other guys around you at the same time."

Dixon shrugged. "I don't know any different. It's all I've ever done." He blew out a breath. "But, if you want the truth, I look at players like you, guys that still enjoy what they do, and envy them."

Tucker's mouth fell open. He slowly closed it back. Though he'd guessed that Dixon lost the fun side of the game a while back, to hear him admit it made it all real. "I'm sorry your father poisoned the sport for you."

"It could be worse. I could have been without a father or had an abusive one." Dixon took another drink. "In the scheme of things, a perfectionist and baseball-obsessive guy isn't the end of the world."

"Yeah, but life's too short to be miserable." Tucker studied Dixon. "I know you're just going through the motions, just like living on an assembly line. You're like the guy who puts a nut on a bolt all day long. It's important and he's great at it, but that's all he really does day in and day out."

Dixon frowned. "I'm the guy that puts a nut on a bolt?" He snorted. "Gee, thanks."

Tucker held up his hand. "Okay. Bad analogy, but you get my point. You need to find something to either make the game exciting again or to switch gears."

For a long moment, Tucker didn't think Dixon would respond. A tendril of fear curled through him, thinking he'd pissed Dixon off, which wasn't his intention at all.

"I've been thinking lately about that." The whispered words were filled with tentative caution.

"That's a good start. Did you come up with any ideas?"

"Coaching." Dixon said the word with confidence as he turned back to the TV screen.

"I can see that. Hell, you've helped me a ton just in a few short days. The other guys look up to you and have been taking your observations and advice to heart. It's improving their outings too." Since Dixon had been riding the bench with his injury, he'd been holding little instructional sessions with the other players who were interested in picking up a few pointers. The rookies were always there and most of the seasoned players listened in, even if they didn't crowd around Dixon. "You have a talent and a way with the guys, that's for sure." The more Tucker thought about it, the more he knew Dixon and coaching went hand in hand. "Are you going to do it?"

Dixon rubbed his thumb over the label on the beer bottle. "Maybe. But there're other things to consider."

"Such as?" Tucker knew Banner would snatch Dixon up in an instant and put him to work. Specialty area coaches were a godsend to any team.

"It's not important." Dixon sat forward, placed his drink on the coffee table, and stood up. "Thanks for the beer. I better get home."

Tucker blinked at the sudden change. "Wait. What's gotten into you?"

Dixon waved his hand dismissively as he walked toward the door. "Nothing. I just need to get some rest tonight. We've got practice tomorrow if you're still interested."

"Of course I am. Ten a.m. at the ballpark. I wouldn't miss it." Tucker hurried over and beat Dixon to the door. "But that doesn't explain why you're trying to hurry out of here like the invasion of the army ants has arrived."

Dixon's lips twitched slightly before he sobered once again and clapped Tucker on the shoulder. "Just be ready. I think a couple of the rookies may join us along with some of the assistant coaches. Get in some good ground work with all the extra people." He nudged Tucker aside and opened the door. "Thanks for putting up with me today and for dinner."

"Anytime." Tucker leaned on the doorframe as Dixon walked past, turned, and started down the hallway. Dixon exited the building before Tucker strode back inside, shutting and locking the door behind him, and plopped down on the couch.

"What the hell, Dixon?" For the life of him, he couldn't understand the abrupt departure, but instinctively knew it had to do with the topic of Dixon becoming a coach. He replayed the conversation through his head.

Other things to consider.

Whatever that meant. Tucker rested his head back on the couch and sighed. "Just when I think we're starting to feel things out, something else comes along."

With no idea of how to address this latest bump in the road, Tucker took both bottles, placed them in the sink, then headed to the bathroom for a long, hot shower.

Chapter 12

TUCKER HAD rehearsed what to say to his mother a dozen times since climbing out of bed, all to no avail. None of the phrases really sounded all that good. Still, he needed to get some things off his chest when it came to his relationship with his mother and how he'd treated her through the recent years. He couldn't wait another day just because he didn't have the perfect words figured out.

Quit beating around the bush and just do it.

He picked up his phone, found her number in the contacts list, then hit the Send button. She answered on the third ring. "Hello?"

"Hi, Mom."

"Tucker. What's wrong?" Worry laced her voice.

"Nothing. Everything's fine." He grimaced when he realized she'd always been the one to call him. So when he initiated contact, of course it would alarm her. "I just wanted to talk to you. If you have time."

"I do."

He heard her chew and swallow as if she was in the middle of breakfast. "I've done some thinking and finally figured out some things. I've been acting like a spoiled brat instead of a man. You bent over backward to raise me, and I treated you like crap. I'm sorry."

Silence answered for a long moment.

"Mom?"

"I'm here. You have nothing to apologize for. I basically tossed you out into the world and told you to make it or not. That's a pretty rotten thing for a mother to do." Regret and shame easily carried through.

"No. Mom. Listen. You left your family and the only support system you had to protect me. Worked your ass off to give me what you could. Yeah, times were hard, but you did everything in your power to take care of me. I never went a day without knowing I was loved despite my mixed heritage." He sat on the couch and leaned forward to rest his elbows on his knees. "I'm so sorry for being resentful. I was so fixated on your leaving after dropping me off at college that I couldn't recall all the years of sacrifice you gave to get me there."

Her breath caught, and then there was the unmistakable sound of crying. His heart plummeted. "Please don't cry, Mom."

"Oh, Tucker. You don't understand. I'm not sad. Your words, they're a dream come true to me. I always hoped we could still patch things together. Be a team like we used to be. I feared I'd hurt you too badly to ever really be your mother again."

"I was the blind one. But no more." He felt his own eyes well up. "You'll always be my mom. I just had to grow up enough to really see the truth. You gave me life and protected me all those years. No mother could have done better."

"I just wish it was more." She sniffled.

"Hey, it turned out okay," he soothed. "I'm following my dream and you're back with your family."

"You're my family too."

The statement hit him hard in the heart. "Yeah, I am." He tried to move the conversation to a more chipper note before he ended up bawling like a baby as well. "I might be quirky and goofy, but you're stuck with me."

She laughed. "I wouldn't trade you for the world."

"Thanks, Mom." He sighed happily. "If you're sitting down, I have more news."

"Uh-oh. This sounds serious."

"Don't worry. It's nothing bad." He gathered up his courage. He had no clue what his mother thought of bisexual people or their lifestyle. Yet, he knew he had to put it out there. There was no point of reconciling if she couldn't accept him for who he was.

"Is this about your baseball career?"

"No, but I'm working hard to earn back my starting position. One of the guys on the team is helping me with extra coaching and practice. Some of the others are joining in as well. We're all benefiting."

"That's great to hear. You've got so much talent, you'll be back starting at second base before you know it." Her confidence in him boosted his ego.

"Thanks. I intend to do whatever it takes to get there. But, that's not what I was going to tell you." He ran his free hand through his hair, hesitating now that the moment had come. "The guy who is giving me private lessons... well... we're lovers."

Technically, they'd only slept together once, but Tucker didn't really want to get into the minute details at this moment. Besides, he and Dixon had an understanding. Slow but steady. They'd get back to that point. Tucker knew it deep down.

"Okay." She sounded a little surprised, but he didn't detect any hint of disgust. "I thought you were dating women?"

"I was. It's just that Dixon and I sort of clicked. I don't know how to explain it."

"Bisexual, but only for this guy, huh?" She paused a second. "Sounds like he's pretty special."

"He is." Tucker caught himself smiling just talking about Dixon, then sobered as he dug down further. "What do you think about me being bi? Does that upset you?" He waited with bated breath for her answer.

"Why should it? You're who you are, Tucker. I would love you even if you had three arms, a hot pink Mohawk, and had a freaky obsession with mud puddles."

He chuckled at the image. "That's a lot of love."

"You don't think I stopped loving you when you grew up, did you?"

"I used to think so."

"Nothing could be further from the truth, son. I did everything for you that I could. I knew you'd succeed if only you could focus on baseball. But, you couldn't do that if you were worried about me paying rent and putting food on the table. That's just the kind of kid you were. It broke my heart to do it, but I left so you could focus on yourself and your dreams. That's not something you could have done within the pack and with me still in the picture. Don't you see? I refused to drag you down. Instead, I let you free to fly."

Memories flooded his mind. His mother encouraging him, always being there, upbeat despite their squalid living conditions. She worked extra hours to send him to baseball camp and never once complained about their lot in life.

The waterworks threatened again. "Oh, God. I didn't know." He wiped at a single tear that trickled down his cheek. His heart ached at the way he'd treated her after she'd given up her own life just so he had a chance at his one and only dream. All the wasted years of despising her. "I'm such a fool."

"Mothers don't stop loving their children when they become adults. Tucker, I understood your animosity with me. You had every right."

"No I didn't. I...."

"You were hurt and abandoned. I hurt too. But, never a day goes by that I don't think of you, watch your games, or follow your career online."

"I don't know what to say." Tucker reeled from the revelations.

"You don't have to say anything."

"I love you, Mom." He uttered the phrase for the first time since he stood on the pavement outside his dorm as an eighteen-year-old kid with suitcase in hand.

"I love you too, Tucker."

"DIXON. WANT to give me a hand?" Tucker asked.

Dixon paused, turned, and smiled at the sight of Tucker juggling two huge bags of stuff from the toy store. Hurrying over, Dixon took one of them from him, very happy to have the walking cast off and be back to his normal health again. Oddly enough, he'd missed playing and could finally resume this morning at the extra practice with a few of the guys.

"What do you have in mind today?"

"I figured since the whole team is having practice in a couple of hours, we should take things back to the basics." Tucker grinned wickedly. "Right, coach?"

"Uh-huh." Dixon shook his head as they headed toward the player's entrance of the stadium. "I'm afraid to ask."

"It'll be fun. You remember what that is, right?"

Dixon opened the door for Tucker while considering his question. Fun wasn't a word he'd used in conjunction with baseball for a long time. Sure, winning the championship last year could fit into the category, but day-to-day games rarely did.

As soon as Tucker passed by, Dixon carried his load through to the locker room. He set his bag down near his locker, then proceeded to change into his waiting practice uniform.

At least I don't have to wash my own team clothes. The dirt and grass stains would never come out.

With a small, rueful grin, he quickly stripped down to his underwear.

Out of the corner of his eye, he saw Tucker do the same thing. The sight of Tucker's exceptional body snared Dixon's attention and made his desire levels jump. *Damn. I still want the guy. Bad.*

Which only added a monkey wrench in his idea of a second career. How could he just leave the team, move to who knew where to coach, and be happy? The simple answer was he couldn't. Not as long as they still had a chance.

Tucker started to whistle as he dressed.

How many times had they shared a locker room? Hundreds? Dixon never recalled Tucker whistling before. Especially what sounded like "Oops, I Did It Again."

Both amused and astonished, Dixon quickly tied his shoes and spun to face Tucker. "You're in a good mood."

"Talked to my mother this morning. Ironed some things out."

"Oh?"

Tucker had mentioned his single mother once before. How hard they struggled and the fact that she dropped him off at college and sped off. "I thought I had it all figured out, with her leaving and all, but I didn't. She did it all for me, knowing that I needed to put all my attention on baseball instead of worrying about her. So, she made a hard decision in order to give me a chance at my dream."

The facts made complete sense. A mother's love certainly. "Wow. That's one devoted woman."

"And I've treated her like shit since. But, that changed today. I'm going to step up and be a better son."

"Great." Dixon squeezed his shoulder. Just the feel of Tucker's bare shoulder sent a small spark through Dixon. He savored it for a second before putting it out of his mind. "I'm glad to see you smiling again."

"I'm getting my life back in order. One step at a time."

"And the next one is earning your spot back."

"Yep." He picked up his glove out of the locker, then the huge bag. "Ready to go?"

"As ready as I'll ever be." Dixon tucked his own mitt under his arm before grabbing his sack and leading the way out onto the playing field.

"Let's leave them here. We'll bring out the goodies after our practice." Tucker leaned his stuff against the wall behind home plate.

Dixon did the same.

"Is there a reason you two are carrying big old bags like Santa?" Ares asked.

Tucker chuckled. "Yeah, there's a reason. You'll find out after we get that extra time in."

Two of the assistant coaches walked over from the dugout area, carrying a bucket of balls, a bat, and a glove. Lance arrived right after them, his playing glove already on.

Dixon gave a brief nod at seeing the players, who gave up their free time and got up earlier than necessary in an attempt to increase their skills. Not all men who made it to the all-shifter baseball league would do the same. Dedicated and motivated, he knew they'd all go far, with the Predators or any other team they chose to sign with. They might be rookies, but they had their heads on straight.

"Field practice first. I'll hit some balls if you guys take positions," Steve, one of the assistant coaches, instructed. "Lance, take first. Ares, short." Tucker jogged to second and Dixon resumed his normal spot at third.

"Here we go." Steve tossed a ball in the air, then hit it with the bat. Hard.

Tucker dove to his right, trapped the ball under his glove, came up to his knees, and fired the ball down to first base.

"Nice job," Dixon remarked with a grin.

Tucker shot him a smile as he stood and brushed some of the dust from his pants.

Just the quick glimpse told Dixon that Tucker was slowly getting his moxie back. Good thing, as he'd missed Tucker's swagger. And his smile. And his hot body writhing in absolute pleasure under him.

The crack of the bat pulled Dixon from his thoughts just in time to duck as a line drive flew straight for his head and past. He turned around and jogged after it since their practice lacked a left fielder.

"What was that?" Tucker asked when he returned to his spot.

"Survival." Dixon tossed the ball back in.

Tucker grinned slowly. "That's what happens when you daydream. Get your head just about taken off."

Dixon flipped him off.

Tucker laughed, then settled into his waiting position for the next one.

An hour and a half later, Tucker headed over to the bags, pulled the items out, then started assembling them. They'd finished the extra practice and headed in to the dugout for some cold drinks and a bit of rest before time for team practice arrived. Tucker didn't bother to sit. He'd just drunk a bottle of water before hurrying over to his stuff and getting back to work setting up a T-ball set.

Unsure why Tucker had purchased such a thing, Dixon walked over, his curiosity demanding he find out the reason.

Tucker finished the task, placed one hand on the stand, and rocked it seemingly to check for balance and sturdiness.

"What's that for?"

"Since Banner would probably have someone's head for throwing some pitcher's arm out, I thought we'd really go back to the starting gate."

"T-ball." Dixon chuckled. "At least I've learned which direction to run the base pads since I last played like this." He vaguely recalled learning how to hit using a device very similar to what Tucker had just constructed, although with a real baseball on top, not a plastic ball, and certainly not short, clunky plastic bats.

"I sure hope so." Tucker grinned. "I'm going to call it Big League T-ball."

"Sounds about right." Dixon picked up one of the skinny yellow bats, noting it weighed next to nothing. "Wonder how many of these will end up busted with the guys going to town with them?"

Tucker frowned. "They better not. No bats, no game."

"Then we better nip that in the bud. Rules are a good starting place." Dixon thought for a second. "Bust a bat and you're out of the game?"

"That works. Same with the balls. It would really suck to play for five minutes, then call the game due to equipment failure."

"Yeah. Just have to defer the grand slams for bunting." Dixon tossed the bat up and down with one hand. "Ought to be fun."

"What in the hell?" Ares approached with his mouth gaping open.

"Who's this for?" Steve asked.

"Why for all of us, of course." Tucker set the plastic ball with holes on top of the tee. The ball was the same size as a baseball, though tons lighter. "We're going to play a little T-ball before official practice."

Lance blinked, then laughed. "You've got to be kidding."

"I never kid about fun." Tucker grinned. "Who wants to be first to hit while the others man the field?"

"I'll do it." Lance took the bat, shook his head at the small size, then lined up next to the tee.

"Just remember that stuff is plastic. While it might not cost an arm and a leg, it's easily breakable. Bust all the stuff and the fun is over before it begins," Tucker advised as he hurried back to his position.

"Got it." Lance took a practice swing, then hit the ball square. It flew over the pitcher's mound and up to second base where Tucker collected it and tossed to first, beating Lance there by a step.

Lance pulled up with a huge grin on his face. Though out, he seemed to be having a good time.

Dixon noticed the same expression on the rest of the guys' faces.

"What in the world...?" Ram approached.

"We're playing T-ball today?" Wiley asked with a hint of excitement in his voice.

"We must really suck if we're doing that." Trigger, always the realist and downer in the group, walked in with Graham.

"Hey, I think it looks like fun." Graham nudged Trigger. "Quit being so cranky already."

Trigger rolled his eyes. "I'm not cranky."

"Yeah, you are."

"Am not."

Dixon rushed over and collected Lance's discarded bat. "Who wants to bat first while the others field?"

"I'll do it." Trigger snagged the plastic bat, which looked like an extra-long butter knife compared to the mass of the big grizzly shifter.

"There's a penalty for breaking the bat," Tucker warned.

"Yep. It's an automatic ejection from the game since there's only half a dozen bats for us to use," Dixon added. "You've got to go easy. No grand slam swings. Think small ball."

"Who has small balls?" Wiley called from the sidelines.

Dixon flipped him off.

Ram cut Dixon a look. "You're in cahoots with him now?"

Dixon grinned. "Yeah, I guess I am."

"Scary, Foxx. Really scary." Ram belied his firm tone with a rueful smile.

"Save us from the canine capers already." Trigger grumbled, but Dixon saw the hint of a smile on his lips as he peppered the ball between first and second base.

Instead of running, he tossed the bat to Graham. "See if you can beat that."

"Challenge accepted." Graham caught it, then dropped his glove to the ground.

Dixon caught the ball Lance tossed in and placed it on the tee. "It's all yours." As he stepped out of the way, Banner approached. The man's face was as unreadable and stoic as always.

Banner stopped next to Dixon and stuck his hands in his back pockets while watching the field. "I knew at some point in my career, I'd return to Little League. Just didn't figure it would be today or all the way to T-ball."

Dixon smiled, then burst out in laughter as Graham smacked the ball. Tucker dove for it only for the ball to stop three feet from his glove. He stood up, walked forward, and picked it up.

Wiley bent over, guffawing at Tucker's expense.

Tucker strode over and bopped Wiley in the back with the ball.

Wiley didn't stop. Not even when Tucker removed Wiley's ball cap, stuck the lightweight ball inside, then placed the cap back on his head.

Hearing chuckles, Dixon swiveled his head to see Banner grinning from ear to ear.

Dixon joined in, enjoying the antics for what they were. Grown men tapping into their boyhood silliness. No umpires or opponents in sight and Dixon was having the time of his life.

All thanks to Tucker.

Chapter 13

DIXON SIGHED in frustration as he walked back to the dugout, bat in hand. He'd struck out. Zero for three so far in the game. A lousy outing. At least he wasn't alone in his misery. None of the other Predators had been able to figure out the top-notch pitching of the Grand River Team. The starting pitcher, Groupers, blanked them and continued to do so.

He'd done his homework but didn't expect Groupers to be so unhittable. On paper, he appeared good, but not great. In real life, he'd proven to be much more than that.

As soon as he trotted down the stairs and slid his bat into the slot with his name attached, he glanced down the bench. All the guys were quiet, heads down, frowns on their faces. The game was fun, unless you happened to be on the team losing six to nothing. Then, it was a matter of getting the punishment over with and moving on. Only a miracle would get them back in the game with such a deficit in the eighth inning.

Can't win them all.

Still, the spanking stung. Especially as they had lost the last three games, although not by nearly such a margin. They were in a slump and couldn't seem to find a way to pick themselves back up.

"Don't worry about it. Every day can't be perfect."

Dixon glanced up at Mack and offered up a small smile. "True. But, still. Damn."

"Yeah, I know. He's having the game of his life. Unfortunately, it's against us." Mack shrugged, then sat back to rest his back against the bench. "It happens."

"Makes for a shitty day," Ram said as he wiped sweat off his forehead with his sleeve.

"Yeah." Dixon understood completely. When games were close or they were leading, guys were in a better frame of mind. When they were unsuccessful and getting whipped, things were completely different.

"Why can't anyone hit him?" Tucker asked. "He's not been this good before, that I can recall."

"I wish I knew." Dixon studied the pitcher on the mound. "I've been watching him all game long and can't figure it out. This one might take some time and videos to pick him apart." Dixon crossed his arms over his chest. "Or maybe he's just having the game of a lifetime, as Mack suggested. No-hitters are thrown from time to time, sometimes by pitchers other than the highest paid in the league."

Dixon saw Ares wave his bat at a slider, then cuss as strike three was called, making for the third man out in this inning. "No rest for the weary." He grabbed his glove, stood up, and prepared to take the field once again.

"I thought that's supposed to be wicked?"

Tucker's comment sparked Dixon's carefully leashed desire. He turned and grinned at Tucker. "Don't you know it."

"Yep. Now go out there and show them that the game's not over until it's over." Tucker patted Dixon on the rear.

The other guys received the same pep talk and pat. Dixon joined the line filing out of the dugout, taking the field like he'd done a thousand times before. For a split second, he considered the role Tucker had played while relegated to the bench. Fun and lighthearted, he strove to keep everyone loose despite the score.

After Tucker lost his starting position, Dixon hadn't expected him to be such a team guy. Many men would be sour about what happened and grumpy toward others, especially the guy who took his place. Not Tucker. He owned his lot in life and placed the blame completely on his own shoulders. Now, he embodied the group spirit. Just another sign that Tucker had changed, made progress, and grown up.

If only he can keep it up.

Dixon turned his attention back to the game. Life on the hot corner could change in an instant. He preferred to keep his teeth right where they were and avoid a major head injury from a line drive while he was distracted.

The crack of a bat a couple of minutes later proved the point. He dove to the side, catching the ball before it hit the ground or flew past for a base hit. After smacking into the packed earth to make the grab, it took him a couple of seconds to get his breath back. Slowly, he stood and tossed the ball back to Tyler.

"Great catch." Tucker's compliment came from the nearby bench.

Dixon gave a quick wave of acknowledgment with his free hand.

"Nice job." Wiley took a couple of steps toward him. "You okay?"

Still trying to catch his breath, Dixon nodded.

"Guess that's going to leave a mark," Wiley said.

"Probably so." Dixon managed to spit out, finally feeling like his lungs were expanding normally once again.

The next batter hit a long ball that arced high in the air over left field. Ares sprinted to the wall. Just as he got to the warning track, he leaped, snagging the ball right on top of the fence and robbing the guy of a home run.

The few fans that remained cheered loudly.

Dixon pointed to Ares with a wide grin. The kid had a ton of talent. No doubting that fact.

Ares casually shrugged like the snag wasn't anything big, tossed the ball back to Tyler, then returned to his normal spot in shallow left.

The outstanding play sparked Dixon's optimism. While they might not be able to win the game, that didn't mean they couldn't put a dent in the score or leave a lasting impression. "We're not beat yet." He yelled the statement to the rest of the players, seeing the energy start to pick up in their body language.

Maybe Ares just gave them exactly what they needed—momentum. Inspiration. A reason to believe that despite the long odds, they could make a comeback.

Tyler seemed inspired as well. He took the mound again, faced down the next batter, and threw a strike. One after another. Three pitches and done. Something he hadn't been able to do all game. With that strikeout, the defense trotted in with a little more enthusiasm than they had earlier.

Dixon stood at the railing, watching Ram stride to the plate. Their small amount of impetus rested on his shoulders.

First pitch, he swung, making contact. The little looper earned him a base hit and ended Groupers's perfect game. Not a huge deal, but pride was on the line.

Dixon cheered along with the rest of the guys.

"Think we can do it?" Tucker stepped over to stand next to Dixon.

"There's always hope. Even though the odds are pretty poor." Dixon focused on the pitcher, trying his darndest to figure out how the guy threw that was putting every single player off balance. Sure, he could pitch some heat, but the movement was what really mattered. The way the ball just dropped off fascinated him.

The pitching coach came over. "For the life of me, I can't figure this guy out."

Dixon agreed. "I've been trying all day long. He's mixing it up, but all his deliveries look identical. Nothing to hone in on."

"Yeah. I'm going to be watching a lot of film later."

"Me too." Dixon hated the fact that a pitcher got the best of him. The attitude had been drilled into him at an early age. All pitchers had weaknesses. It was just a matter of discovering what they were and taking advantage of them. It would come. In time. It always did.

The fact that Cooper, the batting coach, sought him out more times than not stoked Dixon's self-confidence. They seemed to think along the same lines, gave the same advice, and made the same reads. All that information was passed on to the rest of the players to prepare them more for each outing. The outcome of their success depended on it. Dixon understood it more than most.

He also couldn't help but think what it would be like to be in that role full-time. Doing his homework and reporting his findings to the players. The slight change in careers excited him. At the same time, it concerned him. What would make him happy on the field would also potentially sink his social life.

How the hell am I going to choose?

Before he could contemplate the big question further, Tucker edged closer, rubbing his chin. "I think we need something to counter the doom and gloom of this game."

"Not sure the guys are in the mood for another prank." As much as Dixon enjoyed the last couple, he didn't think anyone was in the mood for silliness right now. Not unless the team could mount a rally for the record books.

"Nah. Better than that." Tucker spun around, making a beeline for Banner.

The two chatted for a couple of minutes before Banner nodded and then picked up the phone. Dixon's curiosity was piqued.

"What's up?"

Tucker shook his head. "Nothing."

"Uh-huh. I know you better than that."

"You'll just have to be patient." Tucker offered up a lopsided smile, one that tugged at Dixon's heart. The mischievous twinkle in Tucker's eye didn't hurt either.

"I'm a patient man." Dixon lowered his voice so only Tucker could hear.

Tucker inclined his head in acknowledgment. "Thankfully so." He sidled closer, brushing against Dixon. "How about a movie sometime?"

"Sure." Dixon didn't hesitate a second to answer. They'd been getting along beautifully as friends with the haze of sexual tension hovering over them. He was more than ready to take another step in the direction of progress.

"Tonight?"

"Count me in." Dixon found himself leaning closer to Tucker, drawn in by the small smile on his soft lips.

"Come on, Wiley!"

Shorty's cheer right behind Dixon reminded him of their present location. He blinked and put socially acceptable distance between them.

Tucker glanced down at his shoes, then blew out a breath as he lifted his gaze. "Want to flip for who gets to pick a movie?"

Dixon grinned. "Your idea. You pick."

"Okay, then."

The wicked gleam in Tucker's eyes made Dixon wonder just what he'd gotten himself into.

Before he could get too involved in the query, Wiley made his way into the batter's box. He took a ball, then jumped on the next pitch. As soon as he made contact, Dixon flinched. Sure enough, the third baseman backhanded the hopper, sent a laser to the second baseman. He stepped on the bag and directed the ball to first base while in the process of toppling over courtesy of Wiley's slide right into him.

The small spark of hope blew out after Lance popped up. The game ended on the down note with a shutout.

After gathering his stuff, Dixon followed Tucker into the locker room, ready to pack up and get back home. The early game afforded them the whole afternoon and night to be free and try to recover from such a disappointing day.

"What were you and Banner discussing?"

Tucker held the door to the locker room open for Dixon. "You'll see."

"What's the big secret?"

"Shhh." Tucker shushed Dixon as Banner made his way to the center of the room.

"We have a team meeting as soon as you guys are cleaned up and dressed," Banner announced.

A chorus of discord followed.

Banner held up his hand. "Before you get all pushed out of shape, let me finish."

Dixon waited eagerly, noting the barely restrained smile on Tucker's face. *Whatever had been decided must be good.*

"Tucker's picking up the tab for a steak dinner after we make an appearance at the children's hospital."

"The children's hospital?" Shorty asked.

Banner nodded. "We haven't been there this year. It falls under the category of giving back. Besides, it's a reminder of how good we have it, even on days that we lose."

Dixon embraced the plans. The visits once or twice per year were difficult at times, rewarding always. Seeing the kids, especially those fighting cancer, nearly always broke his heart. Yet, the children seemed to get a kick out of meeting them and receiving the gifts that they always brought.

Speaking of....

"What about the presents? We can't go without some," Dixon pointed out.

Banner turned to answer. "Got it covered. Tucker pointed out there's a toy store not too far away. We'll take the team bus, drop you guys off, let you pick out your own stuff, then we'll head on over.

We're also picking up some stash from the gift shop of Predator gear to sign and give away." He checked his watch. "Time's a wasting, so get a move on."

With such an important event ahead, Dixon made haste in stripping out of his dirty uniform. Tucker did the same, although in front of his locker a few feet away.

"Nice thinking, Tucker."

Tucker shrugged. "Just thought we could all use some levity and a pick-me-up."

"Seeing those kids should do the trick." Ram clasped Tucker on the shoulder. "Thanks for dinner too."

"No problem. A man's gotta eat." Tucker smiled.

Dixon watched Tucker in his element, socializing with the others, and knew that Tucker needed the team. After all, he had nothing else. Unless he counted his mother, who he hadn't seen in years, according to Tucker. That story still made Dixon heartsick to think about.

More than anything, he wanted to see Tucker happy. After the rough years, that's the least he deserved. Whatever it took to make it happen, Dixon vowed to do.

After all, that's what you do when you love someone.

With that thought, Dixon hit the showers.

"THEATER OR home?" Tucker asked.

Dixon slipped on his seat belt and clicked the latch. "Whose home?"

Tucker shrugged as he placed the key in the ignition. "Either or."

Dixon had driven home after dinner. Tucker followed in order to pick him up for their date. No sense in leaving his vehicle in a public place for hours at a time. Too much potential for miscreants to dub it free for the taking.

"I have cable with all the movie channels." Tucker grinned over at Dixon. He didn't mind going out to catch the latest flick, but something about bringing Dixon to his apartment for a private showing sounded more intimate and right up their alley.

Dinner had been exceptional, with all the guys kicking back and enjoying a team get-together. Instead of the dour expressions, they were all smiles and upbeat. The visit to the children's hospital did that for them. Spreading some cheer and gifting those kids with toys reminded them that there was more to life than baseball, at least it did for Tucker. He thought the other guys felt the same as they pledged to visit again and soon.

"Let's go with your place, then. I'm afraid I'm pretty scarce in the movie department." Dixon rested his elbow on the armrest.

"Sounds good to me." Tucker pulled out of the driveway and headed toward his apartment across town. A small thrill rushed through him at the thought of bringing Dixon home.

About time you take Dixon home and get him into bed. The wild dog part of him spoke up out of the blue.

Whoa, puppy. Slow down. It's just a date. Nothing more.

It's a start. A slow one. And about time.

Tucker mentally shook his head at his inner beast. *I'm not rushing into this. No way.*

There's a difference between rushing and moving at the speed of a frozen glacier.

Funny.

"You're quiet. Something wrong?"

Just having a private debate about taking you straight to the bedroom and mounting up is all.

You do want to lick his cock again.

Ugh! Enough about sex already.

Spoilsport.

"Tucker?"

"Sorry." Tucker spared Dixon a glance.

"Are you having second thoughts?" Dixon asked quietly.

"Not in the least." Tucker stopped at a light and turned to Dixon. "I've wanted this for a while, just couldn't bring myself to ask."

"I wouldn't have turned you down." Dixon's lips curled up at the corners.

"I didn't think you would. Just had to get to that place in my head." Tucker's attention returned to the road as he hit the gas again.

"Understood. So what are you thinking so hard about?"

"My wild dog decided to get yappy."

A slight pause followed.

"Does that happen often?" Dixon inquired.

"Quite a bit," Tucker answered truthfully as he pulled into the parking lot of his apartment building. "You know how much wild dogs like to bark." He grinned at Dixon.

Dixon chuckled and unbuckled himself. "I'll take your word for it." He climbed out of the car.

Tucker did the same, making sure to tuck the keys in his pocket and lock the doors behind them.

After opening the door, Tucker ushered Dixon inside. "Want a drink?"

"Got any water? Beer doesn't mix well with coconut cream pie."

"Sure." Tucker locked the door behind him, strode to the kitchen, and retrieved a couple of bottles of water. "Here you go."

Dixon accepted his. "Thanks."

"Have a seat." Tucker picked up the paper movie guide and tossed it to Dixon.

"Hmmm." Dixon thumbed through the pages as he plopped down on the end of the couch.

"Or, there's Netflix." Tucker grinned at the look of concentration on Dixon's face. The grip he had on the brochure, the way he dominated the couch. Everything about Dixon seemed to fit in perfectly in Tucker's home.

"That might be better. I'm not really seeing much here." Dixon handed the papers to Tucker.

Tucker sat down next to Dixon and glanced over the offerings. He didn't find anything of interest either, probably because Dixon snared his attention completely. His heart picked up the pace even as he reined himself in. This was a date, after all, not a fuck fest.

Too bad.

Shut up, he snapped at his inner beast, then turned his attention back to the matter at hand.

"Okay. Netflix it is." Tucker picked up the remote and punched the television on. He scrolled through the options. "See anything you like?"

Dixon turned to face Tucker. "Yep."

Tucker arched an eyebrow. "Why do I have a feeling you aren't talking about a movie?"

"Because I'm not."

Desire shot through Tucker as his libido leaped in response. He drew in a deep breath and met Dixon's gaze. "I'm a mixed breed. Why do you want someone like that?" Tucker needed the affirmation, though he was pretty sure he already knew the answer. Dixon didn't care about things like what mix of genetics a person carried. He saw each one as a whole. Or so Tucker thought.

Dixon traced Tucker's jawbone lightly with his knuckles. "Because you're sexy."

Tucker smiled slowly. "That's it? Just because I have a nice ass?"

Dixon chuckled. "Oh, there's so much more than that." He paused. "You care about others. Always giving. And you know how to have fun. The guys love your pranks."

"Uh-huh." Tucker wasn't sure he'd go that far.

"They do. Keeps them on their toes and loose for the games." Dixon lowered his hand to rest on Tucker's knee. "You're as good on the inside as on the outside."

A small lump formed in Tucker's throat. He swallowed hard at the sincere praise.

Dixon grinned ruefully. "You keep me laughing even as you rev my engine. No one has ever been able to do that before."

"Maybe we should keep it that way," Tucker said softly. The words slipped out, stunning Tucker slightly in the process. He wanted to give them a chance at something important, but being exclusive from now on smacked of commitment. Something he'd always avoided.

The thought sapped some of his desire away.

"I think that's a great idea." Dixon leaned in, found Tucker's lips with his, and plied them with an exquisite touch.

The meeting of lips sent a jolt through Tucker, straight to his cock. He gave back to Dixon, letting the passion free. His worries totally forgotten, he immersed himself in the pleasure.

Dixon edged closer, boldly running his hand over Tucker's chest and down to the bottom of his shirt. He dipped underneath and retraced his path, only on bare skin this time.

Tucker moaned at the sensation. He lost himself in the kiss, then absently dropped the remote onto the couch to free up his hands to explore Dixon's body. Impatient, he shoved his hands under Dixon's shirt, roamed for a bit, then lightly pinched Dixon's nipples. He grinned as he felt them pebble.

"Damn, Tucker," Dixon whispered against his lips before plunging inside once more.

The aggressive plundering stole Tucker's breath. He broke contact, sucked in much-needed air, and closed his eyes as Dixon lapped at Tucker's earlobe. His world narrowed down to the scent of lust in the air, the sound of ragged breathing, and the feel of Dixon's lips teasing his ear.

Dixon dropped one hand onto Tucker's groin.

The aggressive caress through Tucker's slacks brought him up short and in a hurry, just like cold water had been dumped over his head.

I can't do this. Not now. Not yet....

Emotions clashed. He wanted Dixon, physically, but his mind called an abrupt halt. "Wait." He scooted back, took a deep breath, and ran his hand through his hair. "I...."

The sparks in Dixon's smoky eyes died out only to be replaced with a hint of regret and concern. "Too fast?"

Tucker nodded slowly. "I thought I was ready."

"But when it came down to it, you're not there yet?" Dixon straightened his shirt, then patted Tucker on the shoulder. "It's okay."

"I'm sorry." Tucker pulled himself back together by sheer willpower. His cock ached, but its hardness began to dissipate as he grappled with acceptance of himself and what he was. *Gay. No, not gay. Bi.*

"Like I said before, I'm not going anywhere, Tucker. No pressure. I'll be here when you're ready."

The reminder helped to ease the turbulence inside his mind.

He met Dixon's gaze, drawn to the handsome face filled with concern and need. Impulsively, he brushed his lips over Dixon's in a brief kiss. "It's not that I don't want to. Trust me. I just got a case of cold feet."

Dixon smiled slightly. "Cold feet, huh? Well, I have it on good authority that can be cured."

The tension began to ebb from Tucker at Dixon's lighthearted attitude. "Think so?"

"Know so."

Dixon reached around, grasped the remote, and clicked through the offerings. "Now, where were we? Sports or comedy?"

Tucker settled back into the soft cushions on the couch. "Comedy."

"You've got it." Dixon settled on a title, clicked the button, and turned back to face the television. "Just for the record, you throw a great date night."

Tucker snorted. "Hard-on without a happy ending and all?"

Dixon grinned wickedly. "That's just how it goes with dating. Friskiness without completion. All part of the game."

Considering his words, Tucker smiled slightly. "I guess you're right."

"Yep." Dixon took a drink of his water, then stretched his legs out.

Tucker did the same, only placed his feet on the coffee table.

Irony struck him. With his other dates in the past, they always ended up in bed. He now understood that wasn't what he truly wanted or needed. He'd take the girl out to eat, then back for a night of hot sex. Shallow and unfulfilling. It had less to do with getting to know another person and more to do with scratching his itch.

Dixon was different. They hadn't had sex since that first time, and Tucker was still having a ball. That said something. Something big.

Chapter 14

"TUCKER?"

Tucker glanced over at Banner who was posting the batting order on the clipboard in the dugout. "Yeah?"

"You're in." He gestured toward the diamond.

A slow smile crept onto Tucker's face. "The whole game?"

Banner nodded. "Make the best of it."

"Will do."

Thrilled to have another chance to prove himself during a game, Tucker grabbed his glove and trotted up the stairs to the field. He automatically went to his spot, checked out the hardness of the dirt around second base before appraising the grass that separated the outfield from the infield. After all these years, he could get a feel for the way the ball would rebound off the earth or how fast it would scoot through the grass based on the weather and conditions of the soil.

"Welcome." Wiley patted him on the back before walking over to his spot.

Dixon approached with a smile. "Nice to have you back."

Tucker's heart flipped with the sweet grin, the spark in Dixon's eyes, and the genuine happiness on Dixon's face. "Thanks." He scratched at his chest. "It's good to be here." His spot. His team. His home. With the man who made the day that much brighter.

"Have fun." Dixon patted him on the arm and turned.

"Hey, Dixon." Tucker waited for him to face him before speaking again. "Care for another date night?"

Dixon beamed. "Absolutely. Any time."

Even though Tucker knew Dixon wouldn't turn him down, he still felt the surge of relief and thrill when Dixon agreed. Their first one turned out quite well, though they just hung out at his place and watched a movie. A little hanky-panky aside, it was a low-key date between friends. He wanted to step it up for their next one.

"What's this about date night?" Graham asked from just off the mound.

Dixon arched an eyebrow at Tucker.

Tucker drew in air and let the cat out of the bag, so to speak. "Dixon and I are dating."

Graham eyed them both, then nodded. "Good deal." He smiled. "And welcome home. It's always nice to have a great player at my back."

Tucker's spirit soared. "Thanks. It's just day by day, but I hope to be a permanent fixture soon."

"You need to be. Misery loves company after all." Graham wiped at the sweat already building on his forehead.

Tucker chuckled. "I'll bring in an ice truck if you can pull off a rout today."

Graham's eyes lit up. "It's a deal." He returned to the top of the mound.

Tucker moved to his normal spot, catching the ball thrown his direction for warm-ups. He immediately tossed it over to Ram, as was the usual sequence. Task done, he took a moment to take it all in— from the fans to the opponents and everything in between.

This is where I belong.

He'd missed being part of the defense, to be out on the diamond, catching balls, and forcing outs for the other team. It's what interested him in the game initially. Not batting, but fielding. The quick reaction time, the unpredictability of where the ball might go. It all added up to be a fun game. Still was, now that he had gotten his head on straight. To play it with his best friends sealed the deal.

My team. My spot. My home.

He glanced over at Dixon. *And my man.*

The possessive comment came out of the blue but clicked just right.

Dixon met Tucker's gaze and tilted his head as if in question.

Tucker simply smiled.

Fate is a fickle thing, but sometimes she does nail it on the head.

He winked at Dixon, then turned his attention back to the game. "Batter up!"

Tucker focused on the guy coming up to bat, preparing himself by bending his knees slightly and rocking his weight from one leg to the other. A body in motion reacted much quicker than one standing still. In a game of split-second decisions, he needed that advantage.

The batter jumped on the first pitch, sending a line drive up the center of the field between Tucker and Wiley. Though Wiley dove, he couldn't get there in time.

Moving closer to the bag, Tucker prepared to guard his base.

The next man up went to a full count before striking the ball to Wiley. Wiley palmed it on the run.

Tucker was already in motion, dragging his foot over the bag just as the ball arrived. He threw a laser to first even as the runner slid into him. Nothing new as all the opponents did the very same thing. If they toppled him over or interrupted his throw to first, they could prevent a double play. Thus, Tucker pretty much bet on getting knocked down a few times per game. Just another day in the life of a second baseman.

He picked himself up and dusted off his arms and chest.

"Nice job." Ram pointed at him.

Tucker rolled his shoulders, loosening up more. He waved his glove, assumed his typical stance, and stared at the next batter.

The fun had just begun.

Two hours later, Tucker wiped at the sweat mixed with the dirt on his skin and clothes, turning him into a walking grime monster. He'd been in the dirt a few times, diving after balls or being dumped by runners. He'd slid into base twice, once after he hit a double, another on a steal from first to second. Add in a couple of grass stains from sliding after a couple of loopers and he carried plenty of colors to show for his efforts. Looking down at his uniform, he had his doubts that the clothes would ever come clean again. Good thing they received new uniforms each game. Otherwise, he might have a pile of rags to wear after only a handful of games.

He picked up the bat and hurried out onto the field, being the first up in the ninth inning. The score was tied at five apiece. The Predators had the last at bat and thus, the last chance to move ahead, or the game would continue into extra innings.

Considering they were playing against the Stars, Tucker and the rest of the guys wanted the game over with now, as long as it was in their favor. They were rivals with the Stars, and since that team treated Graham poorly in the past, all their current games were personal. No one wanted to lose to those pricks. Pride was at stake. Along with the need to drive home a point to the homophobic bastards.

He'd do anything to kick their collective asses on principle alone.

Tucker waited for the call from the ump, then took his place in the batter's box. He concentrated on the pitcher's glove, waiting for his hand to appear. The second it did, he prepared himself for that split-second decision to swing or not, and where. He let the first pitch go by without moving.

"Strike."

Resetting, he made a mental note of the curve that just nicked the outside corner. Not his favorite position, especially down low, but he couldn't afford to be extremely picky. The release point by the pitcher and the way the ball spun coming out of his hand was the hallmark for the curve ball. Tucker knew a fastball and a slider were also on the board for the guy. What he'd get next was yet to be seen.

The second throw sent him nearly to the ground to avoid getting beaned in the head.

"Shit." He stood back up and wiped his hands off on his pants as he glared at the pitcher. In this level of play, accidents like that didn't happen. Those pitches that put a guy down were intentional.

He snarled at the guy, flashing a fang.

The pitcher smirked.

Anger and adrenaline surged with the basic survival maneuver. He took a couple of deep breaths, gathered himself, and took a moment outside the box to get his focus once again. His teammates began rooting for him and urging him on.

He placed one foot in the back of the box, soon followed by the front one. A single, slow practice swing and he waited.

The pitcher gave a slight nod. Tucker felt more than saw the catcher get into his stance. A second later, the guy drew his leg up, reached back, then threw.

Tucker jumped on the pitch, extending his arms, and swinging with power. The crack and jolt of contact made him drop the bat and speed down the line to first. Along the way, he located the ball, in the left field corner, with a player darting after it. Tucker turned on the jets, sprinted for second. He glimpsed Banner out of the corner of his eye, waving him on. Not slowing in the least, Tucker rounded second and aimed for third.

Banner slammed his hands, palms down. Tucker didn't hesitate, sliding into third base.

"Safe." The third base umpire added in the arm motion with the word.

Tucker held his hand up, asking for time. As soon as it was granted, he regained his feet and tried to dust off this latest layer of dirt.

"Nice hit." Banner clapped him on the back.

"Thanks." Tucker removed his batting gloves and handed them to Banner for safekeeping until he exited the base pads as a runner.

Banner appraised him for a second. "You've stepped up your game."

"A man's gotta do what a man's gotta do." Tucker offered up a small smile.

Banner grinned. "Keep up the good work." He stepped back to the coach's area.

Tucker kept one foot on base for the moment but took a couple of steps toward home once the pitcher had the ball in hand. With a fly ball, he could tag up and dash for home. Any ball on the ground would be an opportunity to go as well. He needed to be prepared for anything.

Milo stepped up to the plate. Banner flashed him the sign for a sacrifice fly. He took his position and swung at the first pitch. The ball shot up, but not deep enough as it never left the infield. The shortstop handily caught it, then stared Tucker down, daring him to try to make a run for it.

Not dumb enough to risk it, Tucker casually stood on top of the base.

He repeated the process through the next batter as Shorty struck out. With two outs, Dixon came up to bat.

Tucker clapped his hands. "Come on, Foxy. You can do it."

Dixon grinned at him, stepped into the batter's box, and turned his attention to the pitcher.

Just a single. That's all we need.

Two strikes later, doubts began to cloud Tucker's optimism.

Dixon fought off bad pitches, fouling five in a row off. The count remained at two balls and two strikes. The next pitch became the most important of the game.

Crack.

Another foul ball. One that almost smacked Banner in the noggin.

Banner ducked in time, stood up, and kept the casual expression on his face as if nothing had happened.

Tucker retreated to third base just like before, shaking his head at Banner in the process. "Good duck."

Banner glanced his way. "Do this long enough and it's a survival skill."

Tucker could understand that idea. Just like with Dixon playing third base, that hot corner, with hard hit line drives coming at a guy in a split second, reaction time made the difference between a hit and an out. Or, at other times, a trip to the emergency room.

He waited for the pitcher to get the new ball in his glove before easing away from the bag, just a few feet, nothing too risky in case the pitcher threw to third in an attempt to catch him off the base.

The pitcher glanced at him, then turned his attention back to the catcher. He spun and sent a laser to third.

Tucker dove back, his hand on the base in plenty of time to beat the tag.

Once again, he stood up, checked the pitcher and took a stride away from the base. It wasn't just about the threat of stealing, it was an attempt to mess with the pitcher's routine, his timing, his mindset. Anything to give the Predators an advantage.

The guy shook his head slightly, then gave a small nod. A second later, he threw.

The ball hit the plate and skipped over the head of the catcher.

Tucker put on the burners and shot for home as the pitcher darted in to cover home plate.

Knowing it would be close, Tucker threw himself feetfirst into the slide, keeping his forward momentum going with everything he had.

The catcher's glove slapped him in the chest.

"Safe!"

The umpire's gesture registered before the word did. The next thing he knew, Dixon pulled him to his feet and into a hearty hug. "You did it!"

Tucker beamed and returned the affection with a quick embrace. Tempted to place a kiss on Dixon's lips, Tucker refrained. In private was one thing, in public totally another.

The whole team filed out to celebrate him stealing home. As the Stars filed off the field, Tucker and the rest of the guys took their own sweet time, waving to the crowd and patting one another on the back for yet another win, this one hard earned over their nemesis.

Tucker found Graham and gave him a big hug. "I owe you an ice truck."

Graham grinned widely. "It wasn't a rout."

"Close enough. You've earned it." Tucker clapped him on the back, found Dixon in the crowd, and walked with him back to the dugout. "Know how to get ahold of an ice truck?"

Dixon's eyebrows furrowed. "Not really, but I'm sure there's someone who does."

An idea struck. "The concession stand. Be right back." Tucker jogged up the steps and weaved his way through people until he found what he was looking for. "I'm looking for the ice truck."

The worker blinked at him, then pointed. "Back door. Down the steps and take a right. He should be there for a while longer."

Ten minutes later, Tucker entered the locker room. He caught sight of Graham and made a beeline over. "Your ice truck is waiting at the player's exit. The guy said if you need him to bring in a pallet, just say the word." Tucker held up his hand, which had a phone number written on it in ink.

Graham's mouth fell open. "How?"

"I have my ways." Tucker sauntered off to his locker. He stopped short when he spied Dixon stripped down with only a towel around his waist. The sight stole Tucker's breath and ramped up his desire once again.

He'd faced this very same scenario numerous times, but this one seemed to be different. He couldn't stop staring and knew the only thing stopping a bulge from showing in his pants was the cup that he presently wore.

At this rate I'll be taking cold showers after all games and practices.

Dixon looked up and caught Tucker's eye. He drew in a deep breath, grinned, and closed the distance between them. "Want to play 'drop the soap' in the shower?"

Tucker bit back a moan.

"Oh, hell. Someone's in heat," Mack said with a put-upon tone as he glanced around the room.

"Oh, shit. Who this time?" Slade asked.

"Last time was damn horrible. Please tell me it's not Trigger. We can't go through that again," Shorty responded.

Amused, Tucker watched Shorty disappear around a corner when Trigger growled menacingly at him and made a quick lunge.

"If it's not the bears again and it's not Ram and me, then who is it?" Wiley asked.

Several pairs of eyes landed on Tucker. He blinked back at them all.

Dixon chuckled.

The sound proved contagious. Tucker laughed with him before grabbing a towel and heading toward the showers.

"Aren't you going to take your clothes off first?"

Tucker paused at Dixon's question. "No way." He didn't elaborate, didn't need to. The fire in Dixon's eyes said he easily read between the lines.

We'll get there. Just a little more time. The thought of being with Dixon no longer rattled Tucker. Instead, it filled him with anticipation and excitement. He wasn't quite 100 percent ready to take the leap of faith as a couple of hesitations still held him back. But each day he grew more accustomed to the idea of his own bisexuality and his unrelenting hunger for Dixon. Each date put him one step closer to the mark.

Not to mention Dixon kept his motor simmering with a smile, a touch. Even his mere presence did the trick. Pheromones and mutual desire told the story.

Things were heating up between them. Big time.

But, this wasn't the time or place to see how hot they'd burn.

Later, though. Definitely later.

Chapter 15

One week later.

PRACTICE WAS gradually coming to an end. They'd been at it since just after noon. Despite there being no game until tomorrow, Banner didn't grant them a day off. Instead, he'd called a full practice to address a couple of "little blips," as he called them.

Unhappy at the loss of a day off, Tucker still couldn't get too upset. After all, Banner had been letting him play more and more. He'd even tossed a compliment in Tucker's direction now and again.

Tucker passed out bottles of water from the cooler as the guys came in from the field, wanting to be useful instead of just sitting around like a bump on a log. He'd been replaced by Lance for the last part of their practice. Suited him fine for today, although he still wanted to be out there with his guys. A week ago, he'd gotten the opportunity to do just that. His appetite for the game had been whetted even more with the taste of what he'd always had until just recently.

At least Banner had made him the exclusive designated hitter for all their recent games. His batting average reflected the extra work, attention to details, advice from Dixon, and Tucker's own determination to earn his spot back. The numbers climbed steadily. His field play had returned as well, though he didn't get nearly as many chances in that department. It would come, he knew, with time. After all, his confidence increased each day as events in his life fell into place.

They'd won their last three games, breaking their slump and putting them right back at the top in the standings. Exactly where they always wanted to be. To boot, they beat the Stars in dramatic fashion, which added to their self-esteem and contentment with their play. Tucker counted that steal of home as one of his best moments in the sport. When he considered how many he'd had over the years, that was saying something.

Dixon trotted into the dugout and accepted one of the bottles from Tucker. "Thanks."

Tucker smiled. "Welcome."

Dixon nudged Tucker with his elbow. "Still up for tonight?"

"Oh, yeah. Nothing can keep me away."

"Good." Dixon casually drifted back to the field.

And this part is getting there as well. He'd been thinking over the past few weeks, probably too much. Spent quite a bit of time analyzing and beating the issue to death. All to no avail. Then, he'd finally decided that Dixon would just be the exception to his straightness. Not a bad choice either. The guy helped him and the rookies by giving up his free time, had become a good friend, and co-conspirator when it came to his pranks. They'd settled into a much more comfortable relationship of friendship. Tucker intended to take it a step further. When the time was right.

Speaking of....

He spied Trigger walking over for a drink. Tucker tried to act as nonchalantly as possible even as he checked his pocket for the blue magic coloring stick. Finding it still there, he sat on the bench and watched Trigger out of the corner of his eye.

Sure enough, Trigger removed his mask, let it drop to the bench, then made his way to the cooler. As he started digging through the ice for his drink of choice, Tucker quickly snagged the unattended mask, rolled the invisible magic paint on, replaced the mask where he found it, and tucked the paint stick in his pocket just as Trigger turned around.

Tucker held his breath as Trigger slipped the mask back on and returned to the field.

He grinned casually and checked his watch. Fifteen minutes to see if the prank worked. And to find out if Trigger was going to kill him when it did.

Banner waved his arm and called an end to practice about thirty minutes later. The guys filed into the dugout, dropping off their equipment as they did so. They all paused to load up on fluids before they'd head to the showers.

Time for the circus to begin.

Sure enough, Trigger removed his mask and tossed it down on one end of the bench. He turned back around, giving Tucker a great view of the bright blue lines across his face where the cushions of the mask rested.

Tucker bit back a laugh.

Mack glanced from Trigger back to Tucker. He arched an eyebrow. "What did you do?"

"Oh, nothing." Tucker prided himself on keeping a straight face.

Mack snorted. "You do know that he's going to rip you to pieces, right?"

"He might try." And he would. Luckily, Tucker was fairly certain he could outrun the surly grizzly shifter, in either form.

Graham walked down the steps into the dugout. He'd spent most of the time in the bull pen, perfecting his pitches. Since practice had been called, the pitchers came in with the rest of the team.

Graham approached Trigger.

Tucker already knew what would happen. He held his breath and waited for the explosion.

Graham grinned widely as Trigger bent over to pick up his catcher's gear that he'd just removed. The erotic spark in his eyes couldn't be mistaken.

Trigger stood up, turned, and faced Graham. He smiled, then sobered as Graham's smile also faded.

"What's that on your face?" Confusion replaced the outright lust in Graham's expression.

"What? Sweat? Grime?"

"More like blue stripes."

Trigger blinked before heading back to the locker room. He returned a few seconds later, with fisted hands and long ground-eating strides. His face scrunched in obvious anger. If that wasn't clue enough, the earth-shaking roar, so reminiscent of his wild cousins, turned everyone's head.

"Tucker!"

"Oh, shit." Tucker leaped out of the dugout, just avoiding Trigger's swipe. He quickly transformed into his wild dog self, shook off his uniform, and hit the gas as Trigger changed into his huge grizzly form. Bears might be big, but they had some speed as evidenced by Trigger quickly catching up. Long, bounding strides and those huge paws, complete with lethal claws, made Tucker take notice.

Tucker quickly revved into another gear and zipped through the outfield, staying just out of reach of the big guy. He glimpsed the rest of the team taking a cue from them. Animals of all shapes and sizes darted around the ballpark. The two bears might outsize the rest of the group but were outnumbered with the various kinds of canines and felines. Some entered in the game of chase. Others sat back on their haunches and watched.

Good thing the stadium remained empty for practice. Otherwise, the fans might get a bigger show than they expected. Along with a lot more naked flesh when they changed back.

The ballpark had turned into a wild animal reserve filled with plenty of playful antics. Tucker caught sight of Dixon zinging around, slowed his pace to watch, only to be rolled by a massive bear paw.

Tucker stopped tumbling when he splatted against the padded outfield wall, pulled himself to a sitting position, and faced Trigger, who was now in his human form. The fact that he was naked didn't affect Tucker near as much as the promise of pain in Trigger's eyes.

Immediately, Tucker shifted and started to talk his way out of the punishment sure to come. "Trigger. It was just a joke. No harm, no foul." He held up his hands in the age-old sign of peacemaker.

Trigger grabbed Tucker's shoulder and smashed him into the center field wall, then held him in place with one large hand to the chest.

Tucker wasn't short by any means, but still his legs dangled half a foot from the ground.

"Trigger. If you rip into him, Banner *will* fire you," Graham reminded in a casual, almost bored voice.

"I'll just break one finger. No, two. Or three."

"Trigger…," Graham warned with a patient sigh.

Tucker squirmed to get free, motivated by the promise of snapping bones.

"What? It's not like he can't shift and fix it." Trigger shoved Tucker back against the far wall again as Tucker managed to gain a couple of inches of breathing room. The padding didn't protect him from the sharp jolt hardly at all.

Graham shook his head and sighed. "You know the longer you stand here tormenting Tucker, the less time we have *alone*. Here I planned on trying out a brand-new fantasy. But, if you'd rather stand around breaking fingers instead…."

Trigger pursed his lips as if thinking hard. He finally dropped Tucker back to the ground.

"This better be washable, asswipe." Trigger growled at Tucker and flashed his fangs.

"Soap and water. Promise." Tucker held up his hands in surrender. He managed to get his legs under him and stand up once more.

"If it isn't, it's coming out of your hide." The warning came with a haughty snort as Trigger walked off, shoulder to shoulder with his mate.

"Noted," Tucker hollered to their departing backs.

Dixon hurried over. "Damn. You're living on the edge, all right."

Tucker grinned mischievously at him. "That was pretty funny, though."

"Worth about getting pulverized?"

"Yep."

Dixon shook his head. "You're such a nut."

"Yep," Tucker agreed.

The spark in Dixon's eyes ignited Tucker's libido. Worries fell away as something clicked into place. He'd been too busy fighting his perception of himself and hadn't realized a few things. Namely, the way Dixon looked at him. Like he made the whole game of baseball happen and caused the sun to rise each morning in his spare time. As if he were the only man on the earth that counted. No one had ever made Tucker feel the way Dixon did in that moment.

Tucker's self-confidence rocketed, as did his need for Dixon, who might still be an enigma, but only he would do.

Ram said to fight his bisexuality was like trying to separate himself from his inner beast. To do so would tear him apart.

He'd been right.

Acceptance brought about a sense of peace and contentment.

Now, he just had to make Dixon see what he saw. Tucker knew his feelings were reflected in his eyes if only Dixon would notice. Tucker went with his gut and pointed to his chest. "Want to kiss my boo-boos?"

Dixon blinked at him, then arched an eyebrow. "Do they need kissing?"

"I think so. Maybe." Tucker bit his lip and waited. Flirting he could do. With women. Men were a novel experience, and he only hoped he'd said something right.

"Well, then. I might be the guy who could help you." Dixon's slow smile made Tucker's heart skip a beat.

"Anyone else smell lust in the air?" Mack asked loudly.

"At least we know who's in heat now," Ram responded.

"It can't be worse than last year," Wiley added.

"It better not be," Milo said.

Tucker flipped them all off before leaning in and locking his lips over Dixon's. "Let's go home."

Dixon flashed a wide smile, took Tucker's hand, and strode toward the dugout. "Want to take a shower first?"

Tucker groaned. "If we stop for that, someone will be screaming for mind bleach."

Dixon laughed. "Good point."

"I don't mind a little honest sweat if you don't." Tucker led the way down the steps of the dugout and into the locker room.

"Not at all. As long as it's you, I'm happy."

The comment made Tucker's heart kick against his ribs.

A record-setting thirty minutes later, Tucker closed the door leading from the garage to the kitchen inside Dixon's house, locking it behind him as Dixon impatiently tugged at Tucker's shirt. As if unable to wait a second longer, Dixon stripped Tucker down, tossing the clothes aside before undressing himself just as quickly.

Hunger and fiery desire struck as Tucker raked Dixon's nude body with his gaze. He couldn't look away, too entranced with the marvel right in front of him. "Gorgeous."

Dixon grinned lopsided. "Nothing compared to you."

The dam burst. Tucker moaned, bracketed Dixon's face, and pulled him in closer for a thorough tasting. He explored and delved, finding nothing as perfect as the taste of Dixon on his tongue.

His pulse picked up speed, as did his breathing. The scent of arousal in the air lashed him into greater frenzy. "I need you. Now." He punctuated his wishes with bold caresses over Dixon's torso and abs. Too impatient to tease, he stroked the warm skin, letting his hands roam anywhere he could reach.

"Are you sure?"

The slight hesitation in Dixon's voice made Tucker pause, but only for a second. "Absolutely. Take me. Fuck me. Mount up and screw me."

Dixon growled and nipped at Tucker's chin.

The command seemed to bring out a more aggressive side to Dixon. Tucker didn't mind, not in the least. In fact, he reveled in the realization that he tested Dixon's control with just a few words. He'd only been like this once before—the first time he and Dixon were together. Desperate. Needy. On the verge of begging for a sample of Dixon's cock.

"Bedroom."

Tucker shook his head as he wrapped his fingers around Dixon's shaft. "I can't wait that long. Right here." He didn't need sweetness or romance. He needed fucked.

"Bend over the couch. Ass in the air." Dixon's gravelly voice spoke of tightly leashed passion about to explode.

Tucker wanted Dixon balls-deep in his ass when it happened.

He strode over to the back of the couch, bent over, and rested his forearms on it. "Now what?"

"Lube. Don't move." Dixon hurried down the hall to the bedroom, his jutting erection bouncing the entire way.

Tucker grinned at the sight, knowing he'd never tire of that particular image. Nor of Dixon's powerful rear as each step caused the muscles to snap.

A moment later, Dixon returned, already rubbing the slippery substance over his big cock. He also carried a washrag.

Absently, Tucker realized that Dixon had taken a moment to wash his hands and face. Probably a good idea considering how dirty they'd gotten during practice.

Dixon passed the warm washcloth to Tucker who immediately wiped down briefly as Dixon stopped behind him. He trailed his fingers along Tucker's crack, then dipped inside.

Tucker jerked at the sudden invasion. The cloth dropped from his fingers and to the floor. A small burn accompanied the addition of two fingers, but quickly dissipated as Dixon pressed inward and downward, bumping his hot spot.

"Oh, yeah."

"Spread," Dixon ordered.

Without question, Tucker did as bidden. Dixon rewarded him with a deeper penetration. Dixon cupped Tucker's balls, weighing and rolling them, sending a quake through Tucker. At the same time, he slipped another digit inside.

Full, Tucker lowered his upper body and bowed his back. He wiggled as Dixon finger-fucked him at a sedate pace. Too slow and too gentle. "Now. Dixon. Fuck me. Now." He groaned as Dixon lightly smacked his right cheek. The tiny sting whetted his desire even more.

Dixon removed his fingers. A split second later, Tucker felt the tip of Dixon's cock kissing his hole. He barely had time to brace himself before Dixon thrust hard, pushing in deep.

Tucker gripped the couch, holding on tight, as sharp pain accompanied the penetration. He jumped, sucked in air, let out a grunt, then rested his forehead on the material.

"Okay?" Dixon paused and rubbed his hand over Tucker's back. The other slipped underneath to strum Tucker's cock.

The sensations merged into a spicy mix of heady pleasure. Tucker lifted back up, arched his back, and peered underneath to glimpse Dixon rubbing his cock. Passion fired on all cylinders once again.

"Yeah. Now get to work."

Dixon chuckled. "Topping from the bottom. How did I know that would be the case again?"

Tucker appreciated the humor but was too focused on Dixon's cock buried in his ass to think of a retort. Instead, he moaned and pressed back to meet Dixon's next thrust.

The pace went from cautious to frantic in a matter of a couple of minutes. Dixon released Tucker's dick and grasped onto his hips instead. For leverage or power, Tucker didn't know or care. He missed the touch, but Dixon made up for it in technique and fast jabs.

Grunts and moans filled the room. Restless with need, Tucker absorbed the strokes, gyrated his hips, and sought a way to slow his rocketing journey to the pinnacle. It wasn't happening, not with Dixon powering in and out.

Their bodies slapped together in a rapid rhythm. Over and over, Dixon surged, nudging Tucker ever so close to release.

A low growl and Dixon's chest covering his back warned Tucker a split second before Dixon's teeth bit down into the flesh on his shoulder.

Tucker howled at the sting that shot him right over the edge. He jerked as pulse after pulse of rapture raced through his body. All the while, Dixon held him tight—with his hand, his stance, and his bite.

Mate.

The single word from his inner beast sealed the deal in Tucker's eyes. "Mine." He didn't realize he'd spoken the word out loud until Dixon growled low in his throat.

Dixon removed his fangs and licked the area, tender where he'd been rough before. "All mine."

The words of ownership put a smile back on Tucker's face. He soaked up the moment, remaining still as Dixon's swollen knot held them together.

Time meant nothing in that moment. Nothing except the glorious sensations that continued to sweep through Tucker until his breathing finally returned to normal.

Dixon released him and pulled out after the gland had returned to its usual size. A feeling of emptiness followed.

"Wow." Tucker stood up, working the kinks out of his back.

Dixon seemed unable to stop petting Tucker. He ran his hands over Tucker's body and peppered kisses across his face. "You liked?"

"Uh-huh." Tucker reached down to lightly trace his fingers over Dixon's partially erect cock. "Talk about fast recovery time."

Dixon grinned wickedly. "I was always an overachiever." He inclined his head toward the bedroom. "Up for another round?"

Tucker's horniness surged back to the forefront. "Nothing could stop me." He took Dixon's hand and walked beside him all the way, a true smile on his face.

He'd finally found what he'd been searching for all these years. *Love.*

Just as he opened his mouth to share his feelings, Dixon took advantage, pushing his tongue inside.

First things first. I'll just have to tell him later.

Tucker filed that promise away and gave himself over to the mind-blowing kiss.

Chapter 16

SUNLIGHT STREAMING in the window woke Tucker. Momentary confusion had him frowning before his nose picked up a familiar scent—Dixon.

Opening his eyes, Tucker found himself facing Dixon as they both shared the same pillow on his bed. Their knees touched, as did their arms. Both naked, they'd somehow lost most of the sheet during the night, leaving a good portion of their bodies on display. Tucker checked out Dixon's prime body as he slept. Muscular. Powerful. Add in the boyish dimple in his chin and the relaxed expression of lazy contentment on his face and Tucker's heart melted.

Just the way I want to wake up every morning. With Dixon next to him after a night of passion. They'd started in the living room, continued in the shower, and finally managed to make it to the bedroom for a final round before they collapsed in exhaustion. Too tired to do anything more, they ate and crashed for the night.

Glancing down, Tucker noticed Dixon's morning wood, standing at attention as if saluting the day. A damn sexy sight, for sure.

Tucker grinned even as his libido sat up and took notice. Everything fell into place, bringing with it peace, complacency, and downright happiness.

Home.

The word rang true. Tucker knew he'd finally found his rightful place.

Tucker had never belonged anywhere before. Preston had been the closest thing to home, even when he considered his youth and college rolled into one. Now, he knew it wasn't necessarily the city, but the people who made this place what it was. More than that, Dixon showed him what it meant to be loved. Supported. Part of a family that supported him no matter his genetics, his batting average, or even his silly pranks.

He sighed happily and snuggled against Dixon's chest. Another novelty—cuddling. He'd never been one to wrap his body around a woman after sex before. Instead, he normally excused himself to the bathroom or rolled over and tried to go to sleep. Anything to avoid that show of affection because his heart hadn't been involved. Now, he knew the difference and reveled in the afterglow, tangled limbs and all.

Love made it all better.

The term no longer sent chills zipping down his spine. Instead, he embraced the newfound emotion, knowing he'd struck gold in the relationship category. Dixon embodied everything he ever wanted in a mate, though Tucker never once thought he'd find that in a man. Now that he had, he wasn't about to let go.

Dixon sighed and stretched.

Tucker peered over as Dixon's eyes fluttered open. *My mate.* He knew it to his very marrow. His inner beast barked in agreement.

Blinking, Dixon's gaze met Tucker's. "Good morning."

Tucker grinned. "Morning to you too."

"Why do you look like the cat that ate the canary?" Dixon arched an eyebrow.

The action and comments struck Tucker as amusing. "Oh, I don't know. Maybe because I have this sexy stud in bed and I've got a whole lot of ideas about what to do with him." He waggled his eyebrows.

Dixon's sleepy eyes sparked. "A lot happened last night."

"Yep." Tucker read the hint of hesitation in Dixon's face. "A lot of good things." When Dixon didn't say anything more, Tucker threw out another line, wanting to reassure Dixon while easing up the tension between them this morning. "You do know opposites attract, right?"

"I've heard that." Dixon turned more to his side, propped himself up on his elbow, and rested his chin on his hand. His lips thinned into a line. "But I'm not a redhead." Dixon's face scrunched into a scowl with the comment.

"You're also not female. But I'm not holding it against you." Tucker smiled wickedly before leaning in to brush his lips over Dixon's.

"Gee, thanks." Dixon grumbled but ended up grinning just before sealing his lips over Tucker's.

The thorough kiss, filled with unsaid emotions and passion, left Tucker breathless. When they broke apart, Tucker met Dixon's eyes. "I love you."

Dixon's expression softened. "I've been hoping you'd feel that way for a while now." He brushed his hand over Tucker's cheek. "But I still love you more."

Tucker chuckled. "I have a feeling no one will ever win that particular argument."

Dixon shrugged. "So, we'll just have to prove it. Over and over again."

Tucker's spirit soared with joy at hearing those words. "Are you sure you want to keep me?" He bit his lip and waited. There were things to consider, namely his lack of purebred genes, especially the domestic dog part. Society was up in the air about crossbreeds in general. To carry the DNA of a pet ranked pretty much the bottom of the totem pole and incited disgust from many.

"Absolutely. You're mine and no one is going to take you away." A low growl of authority carried in Dixon's tone. "Mate."

"The road runs both ways." Thrilled with the declaration, Tucker held it close to his heart. "Mates." The word rolled easily off his tongue.

"Yep. Don't forget it." Dixon smiled. "Better yet, I promise to not *let* you forget it."

"I never thought I'd find anyone who could complete me, accept me and my mixed heritage." Tucker's eyes welled up. He pushed through the emotions, needing to put everything out in the open. "I couldn't see what was right in front of me all along. But, I vow that nothing will drag us apart. Ever."

Dixon nodded, then sobered. He sat up and scrubbed his face with his hands.

Tucker followed suit, in concern. "What is it?"

"Nothing."

The word poked at Tucker's annoyance. "You said that before. Now spill."

Dixon turned his head to peer at Tucker. "I've been thinking about coaching."

"And I said you'll be a great one. Look what you've done for me and for some of the other guys."

"It's not that," Dixon said quietly.

"Then what is it?"

"There're no open positions with the team. I'd have to look elsewhere." He met Tucker's gaze. "College, other pro teams. Minor league." Dixon blew out a breath. "I'd have to relocate in order to coach."

"Have you talked to Banner?"

"No."

"Why not?" Tucker read the parted lips and the steely expression on Dixon's face. "Pride is holding you back."

"I don't want him to think I'm no longer able to play and just begging for a way to stay with the team."

Tucker snorted. "There's no way in hell he'd think that."

Dixon shrugged but didn't say anything more. His shoulders slumped as he stared at the far wall.

Tucker finally understood why Dixon had clammed up about his wishful career change. To follow his dreams, he'd most likely have to leave the Predators, possibly even the area as he searched for a team in need of a batting coach.

The realization stung slightly, but Tucker shoved it aside. After all, he wanted Dixon happy. If that couldn't be found while playing baseball, then they'd have to make do with other opportunities. The Predators might be his family, but Dixon was his mate. There was no contest.

Tucker took Dixon's hand in his, giving it a squeeze. "We'll figure something out. Together."

Worry clouded Dixon's eyes.

The sight drew out Tucker's protective instincts. "It'll work out. Just you wait and see."

"I wish I had your optimism."

"Hey. I just found my mate. You think I'm going to let you dash off to some other team and spend your days checking out other guys?" Tucker added plenty of teasing to his tone.

A small smile hovered on Dixon's lips. "You wouldn't have to worry about that. The only man I want to check out is you."

"Keep it that way." Tucker nuzzled Dixon's cheek. "Because I've fallen head over heels and can't imagine life without you by my side every day."

"I won't jeopardize your position on the team," Dixon retorted. "You've worked so hard to get it back."

Tucker bopped Dixon lightly on the tip of the nose with his finger. "We'll cross that bridge when we get there. First things first." He leaned in to lick over Dixon's lips. "I'm hungry for my mate."

Dixon's breath caught. "How hungry?"

Tucker chuckled while dropping his hand to Dixon's groin. He found Dixon's morning wood and began to stroke. "Really, really hungry."

Dixon's groan told the whole story. He wanted Tucker just as much.

Tucker shoved their problems to the back burner. Right now he intended to put a big smile on Dixon's face in an age-old way—making love.

DIXON CUPPED the back of Tucker's head and pulled him in for a kiss. Sweet and coaxing, he teased rather than demanded. Encouraged rather than insisted. Each touch with his hand was light and precise. Gentleness in direct contrast to the frantic hardcore event of last night. They'd ridden the dragon of lust last night. This morning, Dixon preferred the exact opposite.

He wanted to savor Tucker, to experience something novel for them both. As he found Tucker's cock and began stroking, Dixon made an impulsive decision.

"I want you to take me," he whispered against Tucker's lips.

Tucker leaned back and stared at Dixon, his lips parted, as a flare of excitement appeared in his eyes. "Are you sure?"

Dixon grinned at Tucker's obvious astonishment. "Yeah, I'm sure." Unable to resist, he pressed a kiss to Tucker's nose. "Don't you want to top?"

"Well, I...." Tucker licked his lips.

"It's up to you, but I would really like it if you would fuck me. No, scratch that. Make love to me, but you can call it fucking me if you want." Dixon arched an eyebrow and waited.

Tucker's breath caught before a slow grin covered his lips. "Talked me into it."

"Good." Dixon rubbed his thumb over the top of Tucker's dick, catching the drop of moisture as it emerged. He nudged Tucker to his feet, then bent over to take Tucker's shaft into his mouth. A groan rewarded him.

"Yeah. Oh, yeah." Tucker ran his hands through Dixon's hair, finally settling on leaving one hand to offer guidance.

Licking and laving, Dixon bobbed his head, trying every sensual torment trick he knew. He didn't want Tucker to come, not yet, but needed to give him abundant pleasure in the meantime. A gift. To his mate.

"You're going to make me…." Tucker bit out the words, then stepped back.

Dixon remained in place. "Lube?"

Tucker glanced from side to side, then back to Dixon. "Ummm."

Dixon chuckled. "Don't look at me. Last time I saw it, I tossed it into the sheets sometime late last night."

"Well, hell." Tucker peered under the bed, finally getting on his hands and knees, and reaching underneath.

"Nice view." Dixon's desire shot up at the sight Tucker presented, on the floor, in such a position. A definite erotic inspiration if he'd ever seen one.

Tucker wiggled his rear in response.

Amused, Dixon chuckled while resisting the urge to join Tucker on the floor.

"Aha." Tucker regained his upright stance, holding the tube in his hand.

"That's the one." Dixon smiled ruefully at Tucker. "Ready to try on the top role?"

"Definitely." Tucker's eyes narrowed in the slightest. "Lay back. Put your ass on the edge of the mattress. Legs in the air."

The rapid-fire orders cranked Dixon's arousal that much higher. Without comment, he followed directions, bending his knees toward his chest and letting his legs fall out toward the side. The results gave Tucker easy access.

Tucker squirted some gel on his fingers, then pressed against Dixon's hole. One finger slipped inside.

Dixon bit back a groan at the sensation of being penetrated. He rested his hands on his knees, giving them support while Tucker explored a bit.

Another digit joined the first. A slight sting accompanied it. Dixon grasped his cock and caressed lightly. His aching cock jumped at the additional stimulation, sending a zing of pleasure through him.

Tucker rotated his wrist and met Dixon's gaze. "Like that?"

"Uh-huh." Dixon could hardly form words, too distracted by what Tucker was doing to him.

"You're so damn hot like this," Tucker whispered. He managed to squeeze in one more finger, pumped in and out a few times, then removed his hand completely.

Immediately, Dixon felt the loss.

Tucker moved closer, placed his cock at the entrance to Dixon's body, then stilled. "Watch me. I want to see your face when I take you for the first time."

Dixon's inner fox barked in excitement at those words. He locked his gaze with Tucker's, then sucked in air as Tucker pushed languidly forward.

The burning intensified. He worked his cock faster, trying to even out the two sensations to a happy medium.

"Okay?"

Dixon nodded. He started to throw his head back, recalled Tucker's request, and instead focused on his partner's face.

Tucker tilted his head, exposing more of his shoulder. The action drew Dixon's attention to the mark he'd left behind the night before.

The bite wound—a mating mark.

Powerful arousal flooded his system, shoving all the discomfort to the wayside. He moaned as Tucker pressed deep and deeper still.

Full to the brink, Dixon reveled in the moment. Tucker was taking a man for the first time—him. A pretty nifty fact when you added in Dixon had never bottomed before.

"Oh, damn." Dixon's hips jerked as Tucker pulled back and angled on his return stroke, hitting a hot spot in the process.

"Still all right?"

"Oh, hell, yeah." Dixon grabbed his knees once more. "Fuck me." Tucker only grinned. "I thought that's what I was doing."

"Smart-ass," Dixon growled, needing more, lots more.

Setting a slow pace, Tucker moved with long teasing strokes. Just when he nearly pulled out, he reversed course and thrust to the very depths once again.

A fire ignited in Dixon's blood. He grunted and arched his back more. Anything to get Tucker closer. Harder. Deeper.

Finally, Tucker started picking up the pace—marginally. Still too slow for Dixon's likes, but he didn't have the willpower to do more than lie back and enjoy the ride. Tucker's strokes felt way too good. The expression on Tucker's face way too compelling and addictive to stop.

"Harder. Fuck me, harder." Dixon urged Tucker on.

Tucker offered up a toothy grin. "Demanding mate." He wrapped his hand around Dixon's cock, stroking it in rhythm with his movements.

A few seconds later, he released Dixon's flesh, braced his hands on the bed, and covered Dixon's body with his own.

He lapped at Dixon's lips, trailed kisses down his throat, then sank his teeth into the muscle connecting the shoulder and neck.

Dixon saw stars. He fisted the sheets and held on for dear life. Sweet rapture struck like a bolt of lightning, sending him catapulting into orgasm. One second he pleaded for more, the next, strong crests rolled through him bringing along bright rounds of ecstasy. He came hard. His cock pulsed again and again, coating his chest.

Tucker gave a muted shout, his face scrunched, and his cock swelled even larger. Warm jets quickly followed deep inside Dixon's body.

Joined with my mate.

The words played through his mind as he struggled to catch his breath after such an experience. Unable to move because of Tucker's swollen knot, Dixon relaxed back into the mattress, content to watch the myriad of emotions flashing across Tucker's face. Small intermittent ripples rolled through now and again, a continuation of the rapidly fading climax.

Dixon forgot about everything but Tucker and the pleasures they still shared. He ran his hands down Tucker's sweaty back and nuzzled his cheek, careful not to jar Tucker too much while his teeth were still embedded in Dixon's flesh.

"Damn, Tucker." He blew out a breath as the knot relented, easing the pressure inside Dixon's body. "That's a hell of a way to lose my virginity."

Tucker let go with his teeth and pulled away enough to stare down into Dixon's face.

"You've never been on the receiving end before?" Tucker's mouth fell open.

"Nope. You're my first."

Tucker's eyes widened before a slow smile appeared. "Guess that makes us even."

"More than that. It makes us mates." When Tucker blinked, Dixon added, "Do you think I'd let just anyone tap my ass? I'm a natural top, if you hadn't noticed."

"Well, I hadn't really thought about it."

Dixon kissed Tucker's nose. "Now you know. You're one of a kind and all mine."

In that moment, Dixon knew that dreams come true. For those lucky enough to find their soul mate.

His certainly did.

Chapter 17

"TUCKER?"

Tucker spun around to face his head coach. "Yeah?"

Banner grinned slightly and tossed Tucker's glove to him.

Easily, Tucker caught it.

"Get out there. Take your spot."

Tucker paused for a second. "You mean for today?"

"No. I mean for the season. You've earned it back. Hang on to it."

Tucker's joy muted as he glanced toward Ares and Lance, the two rookies that he'd booted out of a spot, and presently stood halfway across the field. "What about them?"

Banner paused in his steps leading away. "They're in the outfield with Mack." Banner gave a brief nod and walked away.

Tucker let the words sink in and slowly smiled. *I have my starting position back.* He wanted to shout the news to the heavens. To find Dixon and celebrate.

Dixon. With the name came the idea. "Coach?"

Banner stopped and turned. "What is it?"

Hurrying to catch up, Tucker met Banner's eyes. "It's Dixon."

Banner's eyebrows furrowed. "What about him?"

Tucker drew in air and hoped he wasn't overstepping his bounds. "He wants to coach. Badly. But, he doesn't want to leave the Predators. Is there anything...?" His voice trailed off, not sure what to ask for.

"I've been wondering that for a while now." Banner rubbed his chin. "He's taken some of the workload off the assistant coaches and helped out the rookies."

"Dixon got me back into the game. Without him, I most likely wouldn't have made it," Tucker pointed out, eager to throw more testimonials on Dixon's cause. "He's great at scouting out pitchers. Better than anyone I've ever known."

Banner remained mute for a long moment before tilting his head as if in deep thought.

"Any team would love to have him," Tucker added. "It would be a huge loss to the Predators." He nervously rubbed his glove, waiting on Banner's decision.

"Would your asking have anything to do with the fact you're carrying Dixon's scent right now?"

Tucker swallowed a little sheepishly. He wasn't ashamed of their mating but wasn't quite prepared to announce it to the world either.

After a strengthening breath, Tucker gave a short nod. "We're a couple. Love one another."

"That's definitely a switch from your usual dating routine."

"I know. It took me a while to figure things out. To discover the real me."

"And?" Banner asked.

"And, as amazing as it sounds, I love Dixon. We're mates." Tucker didn't need to explain further. Once a couple declared themselves mates, they were paired off for life. Not because of any laws or silly society rules, but simply because to love another person that deeply meant that they made the relationship work—for as long as they both drew breath.

A ghost of a smile appeared on Banner's lips. "I can't make any promises."

Tucker nodded. "I understand. Dixon didn't want to say anything, didn't want to seem like he was begging for a job."

"Got it." Banner spun around and strode off.

Tucker watched him go while sending up a little prayer. "I just found him. Please don't make me lose him now."

We're not leaving Dixon, the inner beast announced with command.

No, we're not. Tucker made a hasty decision, but one that felt right. Wherever Dixon went, Tucker would go too. As much as he'd hate to leave the Predators, Dixon meant more. Feeling peppier than he had in a while, Tucker made his way out onto the field for batting practice.

He collected his bat, then took a position near the wall, watching as Dixon stepped up to the plate.

"Tucker!"

The sound of his name snared his attention. The crowd that arrived early often hollered at players in hopes of meeting them or for an autograph. This was different.

He spun around and searched the stands.

"Right here." She trotted down the steps toward him.

Tucker saw the wave and centered on his mother's voice. The moment he saw her, a lump formed in his throat. His eyes started to well up. "Mom?"

He'd never expected to see her again, especially at one of his games. Not after she drove away, leaving him standing on the sidewalk as a lost eighteen-year-old boy. Lately, he'd hoped they'd reunite but hadn't gotten further than that.

She made her way to the wire netting behind home plate, then frowned.

Tucker motioned for her to move toward third base, then made his way along the barrier until the wire ended and only railing separated the stands from the field. After vaulting over, he trotted to meet her, wrapping her up in a hug as soon as she was within arm's reach.

She squeezed him back.

Tucker heard her ragged breathing and felt dampness on his game jersey from her tears. His own soon followed. Stepping back, he brushed the hair out of her face. "I can't believe you're here." The words broke with emotion.

She smiled. "I wanted to come so many times but wasn't sure how you'd react. This time, I knew I had to be here." She cupped his cheek and brushed away a stray tear of his. "I've missed you so much."

He hugged her again, soaking up the moment he hadn't known he'd wanted or needed until just recently. The sound of familiar men's voices broke into their reunion.

Tucker took her hand in his. "Come on. There's someone you need to meet."

She grinned. "Would this be the man you told me about?"

"Yeah." Tucker beamed and led the way. He helped her onto the field where Dixon immediately met them.

"Mom, this is Dixon. My mate." The term made his heart warm. "Dixon, my mother, Sheila."

"Oh my." She reached out a hand. "Dixon. It's so nice to meet you."

Dixon took her hand gently. "I've heard about the sacrifices you made for Tucker. Thank you. Not everyone has as much dedication and fortitude to do what you did. You're an amazing mother."

She blushed even as she smiled to outshine the sun. "I didn't do more than any other mother would do for their son." She looked back at Tucker. "I should have done more."

He shushed her. "You gave me life, cared for me growing up, then you let me fly on my own. I'd say that was a damn sight above and beyond." He wiped at his face, unashamed of his remaining tears.

Dixon met his gaze with a wide grin before turning his attention back to Tucker's mother. "I'd appreciate it if you'd have dinner with us after the game."

"I'd love to."

"Dixon! You're up!"

Dixon tipped his hat. "Duty calls." He strode back toward the batter's box.

Tucker escorted his mother a few steps away from the action, into a safer place, just in case any balls flew their way.

"Your mate. Wow. I knew he had to be something special when you told me about him." She grinned ruefully. "A mother knows these things."

Tucker just shook his head in amazement. "He's wonderful. Smart. Caring."

"And easy on the eyes."

"That too," Tucker agreed.

The sound of Dixon's voice raised in frustration caught Tucker's attention. He glanced up to find Dixon's father nearby, once again critiquing Dixon's swings.

His face pinched in restrained anger, Dixon snapped right back.

"Uh-oh." Tucker left his mother and hurried over.

"If you'd just do as I told you, you'd be able to hit those sliders better. I don't see why you're so hardheaded when it comes to trying to better your game." Dixon's father fisted his hands.

Dixon readjusted his grip on the bat, squeezing so tight his knuckles went white. "I don't need you always picking me apart. I'm a big boy now and doing just fine." Dixon narrowed his eyes as he stared down his father.

"Not according to your batting average. You've got a tradition to uphold, and you're slacking," Terrance argued back.

Fire snapped in Dixon's eyes. "Slacking? You think I'm slacking?"

Tucker jumped between the two men, nudging Dixon back a couple of paces before Dixon lost control completely and walloped his father with the bat.

Banner stepped into the gap and glared at Dixon's father. "Foxx, you're out of line."

"I'd say so." Tucker's mother entered the fray.

Tucker twisted to keep an eye on her while holding a hand on Dixon's chest at the same time.

"A parent is supposed to love their children, support them, encourage them. Not tear them apart every time they see them." She planted her hands on her hips and huffed. "I don't care who you are or what you've done with your life. Being a parent is more important than all that. But, I guess a man as nearsighted as you can't see that."

"Who are you to criticize me?" Terrance stood up straight, drawing attention to the differences in their size.

Sheila just grinned ruefully. "Tucker's mother. Since he's mated to your son, I suppose that makes us in-laws."

Terrance's mouth fell open.

"A parent loves their child, no matter what," she reiterated.

"He's one hell of a player and an even better coach. When he's ready to retire, he's got a hitting coach position waiting for him," Banner announced. "That's more than you've ever done."

The snide remark made Tucker grin. Banner might be one hard-ass, but he stood up for his guys.

Peeking over, Tucker saw Dixon relax, his grip on the bat loosening as the anger left his face.

Banner eyed Terrance for a few second before turning back to Dixon. "We don't have all day for batting practice, so get moving."

Tucker's mother crossed her arms over her chest, still intent on Terrance. "So, are you going to step up and be a father, or do you prefer to be a jackass in front of everyone?"

Terrance snarled, then walked off.

Tucker's mother huffed, then turned back to Dixon. "I'm so sorry."

Dixon waved his hand. "It's okay. Nothing new for me."

"That's sad." She closed the distance and hugged him. "You're good for Tucker. I'm glad you found one another."

Dixon patted her back and smiled.

Banner offered his arm. "Ma'am. If you come with me, I'll get you to the VIP section so you can watch the game."

"But, my ticket is for section AA."

Banner started walking for the bird's-eye seats next to the dugout. "Not any longer. Parents of players always get the best seats in the house."

Tucker watched them go with a grin.

"That woman has some guts," Dixon remarked next to Tucker.

Recalling the words that flew, Tucker met Dixon's gaze. "Think he'll listen to her advice?"

Dixon glanced in the direction his father took. "I have no idea, but I'm not about to hold my breath."

Ram came over, followed by the rest of the team. "Mates, huh?"

Tucker groaned to himself. The fact was supposed to be their secret—at least for a little bit longer.

Dixon nodded. "Yep."

A chorus of congratulations and cheers followed.

"About damn time." Mack clapped Tucker on the back. "The pheromones were so thick around here my nose burned."

"Yeah, right." Tucker rolled his eyes, then ended up grinning. "Well, maybe."

Trigger snorted. "No maybe about it. It reeked of dog in heat."

"Better than bear in heat like last year," Wiley countered. "That was awful."

Trigger narrowed his eyes at Wiley, then shrugged. Before he walked away, he patted Dixon and Tucker on the shoulder. "I'm happy for you."

"Wow. He's mellowing." Dixon blinked.

Tucker agreed. "Must be what happens when you're mated and pretty damn happy." He sent a wicked grin to Dixon.

"Uh-huh." Dixon smiled in return.

Banner approached as the rest of the team returned to their places for warm-ups and addressed Tucker. "Glad you could work things out. I was pulling for you."

"Thanks." Tucker lifted his chin at the praise.

"I meant what I said about having a position for you whenever you want to try your hand at coaching," Banner told Dixon.

Dixon stilled, then put out his hand. "You don't know how much this means to me." His voice threatened to crack at the end.

Banner took his hand and pulled him into a quick hug. "Now, take your mate and get back to work. We have a game to play today." He gave them one last look, then walked away.

Tucker found himself grinning like a kid in a candy store. "See? I told you everything would work out."

Dixon elbowed him. "I'm not answering that on the grounds that your ego might grow bigger."

"Among other things." Tucker waggled his eyebrows.

Dixon threw back his head and laughed. "Come on, mate. The game waits for no one."

Happier than he ever remembered being, Tucker walked alongside Dixon.

If someone told him three months ago that he'd be not only sleeping with Dixon, but mated to him, Tucker would have offered them a one-way trip to the psych ward. Never would he have expected that his other half would be a man or that he and his mother could find common ground and make amends after all this time. He took a second to reflect on his previous life and saw how shallow and juvenile he'd been.

Now, he'd finally grown up into the man he'd been meant to become.

All because of Dixon. The love of his life and the man who claimed his heart. For now and always.

Epilogue

One month later.

DIXON CAUGHT movement out of the corner of his eyes. He swiveled around to see Tucker wind up the toy rat and release it toward the middle of the locker room. Squeals and shouts followed. A few of the guys sought refuge on top of the long wooden benches in front of the lockers. A couple rolled their eyes and continued changing clothes. Most stared at the vermin drolly, in no way appearing shocked or concerned.

I'd wondered when he'd pull out that silly rat.

Dixon took in the scene, chuckling at the loud stir one little toy caused.

Graham stepped down from a nearby chair, cautiously watching the brown furry thing roll by.

"Tucker!" The whole room echoed in an annoyed chorus.

Tucker tried to maintain an innocent expression, only to lose it as he broke out in great guffaws.

Mack shook his head. Lance lowered the shoe he held up, presumably to kill the interloper. More than one guy shot Tucker annoyed glances as they came down from the perceived protection of the bench.

Trigger kicked the thing as it came close. His lips twitched as he stared at his mate.

"What?" Graham blinked back.

Trigger chuckled. "Don't worry. I'll protect you from the toy rat."

Graham snorted, then flipped Trigger off.

"Later, mate. Later." The smoldering look in Trigger's eyes said it all.

Dixon was just glad they were at a home game so he didn't have to listen to loud, rambunctious bear sex next door all night long.

Tucker dashed by, collecting his toy before one of the guys killed it. After plucking it off the floor, he stashed it back in his locker.

Dixon had no doubts that particular rat would appear once again down the road.

"Quit dallying. We've got a game to play." Banner's voice carried easily through the locker room.

"Yeah, yeah." Wiley blew out a breath as he eyed Ram.

Dixon saw the spark of love flash in Wiley's eyes. He knew it was the same as when he looked at Tucker. He openly showed his feelings for his mate, not caring who ogled them.

At least he didn't have to worry about any of his teammates. They were as supportive as they could be.

"Come on, Foxy. Get your rump in gear." Tucker gave Dixon's posterior a pat as he walked by.

Dixon stared at him drolly. "Keep that up and you'll definitely be late for the game."

"Oh, good grief. Save me from the canine pheromones and lust factory." Mack rolled his eyes and brushed past them both.

"Try it, you might like it," Tucker retorted.

Mack flipped him off, not bothering to turn around or slow down as he made his way to the dugout.

If Tucker got a nickel for every time someone flipped him the bird, he'd be rolling in dough. Dixon chuckled at the thought. He turned and followed Tucker, his gaze locking on Tucker's perfect ass.

"Keep staring and you might burn a hole in it."

Dixon glanced over to find Ares grinning widely. The kid had talent and, occasionally, a wicked sense of humor that probably got him in trouble growing up. Pretty much a requirement for being a shifter, especially one playing professional sports with a whole slew of other shifters. Going with the flow had a whole new meaning when top-level predators were put together in a group and forced to endure one another day in and day out.

Thankfully, just about all the players managed to play well with others.

Trigger didn't count.

"I was thinking more along the lines of committing it to memory."

Ares snorted. "If you don't have that image implanted in your brain by now, you never will."

Dixon shrugged and gently shoved Ares through the door and into the dugout. "One of these days...."

"Yeah, yeah. Just like the arthritic knees and adult diapers." Ares smirked.

"Smart-ass." Dixon tapped him on the arm good-naturedly. "Get out there and earn your keep."

Dixon trotted up the steps behind Tucker. They were just in time to be the last two to pick up the bat and take a few swings at some easy balls.

Batting practice went fairly normally. Dixon smacked a few good ones, a couple over the fence. *If only it were that easy against Groupers.* He'd been working extra, trying to find a way to break down the opposing pitcher and still hadn't come up with much insight.

His turn complete, Dixon exchanged the bat for his glove. Automatically, he walked over to his starting position at third base and caught the ball tossed at him from Ram. Warm-ups were in full swing.

"Heads up, Tucker." Dixon threw a strike to his mate.

Tucker backhanded the ball, effortlessly dragged his foot across second base, and sent the ball on a line back to first.

Yeah, that will do. Dixon nodded in approval. The old team running like a well-oiled machine once again.

After a few minutes, the umpire gave the warning signal that they would need to vacate the field for a little bit for the official reading of the starting players to happen along with a coin toss to determine who started on offense and who on defense. Once that finished, they could retake their places or pick up the bats and get the show on the road.

A motion caught Dixon's attention. He swiveled around to see a few fans on the field. Tucker's mother was one of them. He grinned as Sheila fussed over her son, knowing Tucker had come to terms with the past and found common ground with his mother. They spoke often and seeing them together brought out the obvious love Sheila had for her boy.

Dixon approached them. "Sheila. Nice to see you again." He'd liked the woman from the start, and seeing the wide grin on Tucker's face only sealed the deal in Dixon's opinion.

"Dixon. Please tell me Tucker isn't driving you batty already."

Tucker arched an eyebrow.

Dixon hem-hawed and scratched his forehead. "Well...."

A woman approached from his left. Dixon blinked in recognition. Astonishment mixed with a little concern hit him in the gut. "Mom. What are you doing here?" She rarely attended one of his games, and only the most important ones. Today's game had no significance other than another notch in the win column for the team.

She smiled sweetly. "To watch you play, of course."

He greeted her warmly, happily surprised with her appearance. She rarely attended a game since he hit the pros. That didn't bother him, though. She put tons of miles on the car driving him to practices and games as a kid since his father was out of town a lot during the season. She'd seen more than her fair share of games. So, he couldn't hold the absence against her now.

His father strode over, a stern expression on his face.

Dixon greeted him with a quick nod. "Dad." He recalled Tucker's mother. "Mom, this is Sheila, Tucker's mother. Sheila, this is my mother, Charlotte. And you already know my father."

Sheila nodded. "Yes, I do." Her focus flickered from his father to his mother. "Pleasure to meet you, since we're almost related now."

"I'm so happy for them," his mother beamed at Tucker. "I was hoping someone would come along and steal Dixon's heart away. I'm glad it's you, Tucker."

Tucker offered up a lopsided smile.

Dixon's father stood behind her, looking a little sheepish. He caught Dixon's attention. "You and that shoulder." His father sighed as if in frustration or perhaps, resignation. Dixon didn't know which, nor did he care.

Dixon bristled. "Please, Dad. I don't need any critiques today." He stood up straight and pinned his father's gaze. "For once, can't you just be my father instead of a nitpicky hard-ass coach?"

Terrance's lips parted as he grimaced.

"That's all I've ever wanted in life. Just to be your son. Not your baseball project."

"Why else would I spend so much time coaching you to be the best if it wasn't for love? I wanted for you all the rewards I earned along the way and then some," Terrance answered. "Maybe I didn't go about it the right way, but I do love you. How could I not? You're my son. And a damned good one at that."

"You always want better for your kids than what you had," Tucker's mother chimed in.

"Exactly," Dixon's mother agreed.

"Even if you don't always make that clear," his father said.

An apology if Dixon ever heard one from the man.

Tucker patted Dixon on the back. "Sounds like you're well-liked today."

Dixon chuckled, swallowed the lump in his throat, then hugged both of his parents at the same time, noting the glimmer of tears in his father's face when he stepped back.

"I'm proud of you, son." Terrance ruffled Dixon's hair.

Dixon fought back tears at the affectionate gesture. His entire life he'd waited to hear those words. Now, he couldn't believe they'd actually been said.

"This calls for a celebration. Dinner is on us this evening," his mother announced.

"Thanks." Tucker nudged Dixon, shooting him a happy grin.

"Clear the field, the game's about to start," the home base umpire hollered as he waved his hand at them.

"We'll see you after the game." Dixon's mother gave him a quick kiss on the cheek. He noticed that Tucker's mother did the same.

His father shook his hand. "Figure out Groupers yet?"

Dixon shook his head. "No. He's slick. I've watched him from the first game we played against him and on tape. Didn't pick up anything consistent."

Terrance nodded. "He is that. The key is in the location of his glove. At his chest is usually a fastball. Closer to the belt is a slider. Maybe an inch difference in the two. I doubt he even realizes it. Flat wrist in the glove for the fastball. A little turned is a curve."

Dixon grinned slowly, impressed and amazed at his father's observation skills. "Damn, you're good."

His father beamed and slapped Dixon on the back. "Some habits die hard." He met Dixon's gaze and nodded slightly. "Go get 'em."

For the first time in years, Dixon smiled proudly at his father. He read the expression and in between the lines on his words. His father loved him and, like all parents, wanted to see their child succeed. Once again he was a little kid, wanting to please his father by hitting a clutch home run.

Terrance gave a little wave and followed his wife back to the steps leading to their seats.

Dixon watched him go with a sense of completeness and fulfillment.

"So, mate, going to let me in on the secret?" Tucker stopped next to Dixon.

"I'm happy, Tucker. Really happy." Dixon's spirit soared.

"Game time!"

The call of the umpire interrupted the great moment, but not before Dixon stole a quick kiss from Tucker.

"For luck?"

"More because I love you."

Tucker smiled sweetly. "That's a pretty damn good reason." He led the way down the stairs and into the dugout.

Dixon chuckled, grabbed his glove, and sprinted out to his field position, noting Tucker did the same. He blew out a breath and focused on the game. Life on the hot corner didn't allow for dillydallying. Not if he wanted to keep his head on his neck.

Nine innings later, Dixon's smile had turned to serious concentration as he walked up to the batter's box. Sweat, dirt, and grime stained his jersey, testament to the gritty play in the low-scoring game.

He'd been watching Groupers all game, passing along the hints from his father to the rest of the team. He and some of the other guys had made contact with the ball, but hadn't been able to score, being shut down before any of them could cross home plate. Frustration set in, but Dixon kept focusing on the next bat. Getting more in sync with Groupers. Picking up the subtle hints and taking advantage of them. Now, they were down to their last out and the luxury of time disappeared.

Thankfully, they'd held the Grand River Rivals to only two runs, but that deficit seemed huge in the bottom of the ninth.

Presently, the Predators threatened with the bases loaded. But, two outs tipped the scales somewhat evenly. One strike out, a fly, or even a ground ball could possibly end their chances of beating the best pitcher in the league. Dixon knew the score well. Pressure and tension rested hard on his shoulders under the strain.

"Batter up!"

He stepped into the batter's box, took up his stance, and stared at Groupers. The pitcher held his glove a little high on the chest. Dixon caught a glimpse of the flat wrist. *Fastball on the way.*

Groupers sneered with confidence.

I've got your number, buddy. Just throw it already.

Groupers reared back and slung the ball.

Dixon swung at the pitch coming in around his knees. The *crack* of the bat split the air. Dixon took off to first base, slowing as the ball left the park and dropped into the upper tier stands in left field. A game-winning grand slam. An accomplishment that happened rarely, even to the league's elite. He'd only hit one other one in his career and that was during his college years.

"Yes!" Dixon grinned as he trotted around the bases. He glimpsed Groupers lower his head in defeat, then walk off the mound and toward the visitors' dugout along with the rest of his team.

Excited and thrilled, Dixon focused on his teammates, gathering around home plate. Unable to contain his excitement, he stomped on home plate. The men swamped him, patting him, hugging him, and ruffling his hair. Dixon laughed, pretty damn happy.

The guys stepped back, leaving Tucker standing right in front of Dixon.

Speaking of exciting....

Love and joy reflected in Tucker's eyes. The same expression Dixon knew he wore.

Dixon had found the love of his life after months of pining away, not thinking Tucker and he could possibly become a couple, let alone mates. Certainly his greatest dream had come true. His father had seemingly turned over a new leaf and stepped into the role of father. Add in the fact that the Predators were once again on top of the standings and he'd just won the exceedingly difficult game on a two-out ninth-inning grand slam and Dixon was on cloud nine.

The baseball achievements paled in relation to his mating to Tucker. He smiled at the man he loved more than he'd ever thought possible. "You're the best thing in my life."

Tucker grinned and wrapped his arm around Dixon's shoulders. "I keep telling you that. Glad it's finally sunk in."

Dixon chuckled in humorous delight. Leave it to Tucker to put a sassy twist on his comment.

The years ahead were sure to be an adventure with Tucker by his side. But one thing was for certain—they would be filled with love and laughter.

Together, they walked to the dugout. Teammates. Friends. And mates.

CHEYENNE MEADOWS, while growing up in the Midwest, began reading romance novels in high school, immediately falling in love with the genre, to the point where she decided to write professionally for a career. However, that dream splattered against a brick wall, resulting in a quick death in her first writing class in college when the professor told her bluntly that she wasn't any good at it. She shifted gears quickly and left her writing dreams behind, eventually settling on becoming a nurse.

A few years back, she stumbled across a fan-fiction writing site on a favorite author's webpage. She began to read stories others wrote, not only making some wonderful close friends from the experience, but also, really learning to write for the very first time. Here she was able to share short stories, practice her writing skills, and truly develop into a writer. More than that, the experience allowed her to revitalize her dream as she rediscovered joy in writing.

Now, she spends her days off with her characters, seeing how much trouble everyone can get into. When she's not working or writing, she enjoys playing in the garden, hanging out with her diva kitty, and using her backyard as a living canvas for her whimsical landscaping, and, of course, reading romance novels.

Facebook: www.facebook.com/cheyenne.meadows.10
Blog: cheyennemeadows.blogspot.com
E-mail: Cheyenne1.meadows@yahoo.com

FRIENDS
WITH *Benefits*
CHEYENNE MEADOWS

Shifter Hardball: Book One

Playboy wolf shifter Wiley can't duck out of his pack's biggest annual event, despite knowing his grandmother has possible suitors lined up and waiting. Wiley has no intention of settling down, and the situation dangles just above disaster. Thankfully, Wiley's best friend, lion shifter Ram, agrees to pose as Wiley's boyfriend for the weekend.

They find out fate has other plans when they kiss on a dare, and the passion erupts, so hot and intense they fear the couch may spontaneously combust beneath them. Neither man is able to push the small act of affection from his mind, but both struggle with uncertainty and the ramifications of following where their libidos lead.

If they can't outrun their feelings, they'll have to muster the courage to face their fears before they lose everything, including their friendship.

www.dreamspinnerpress.com

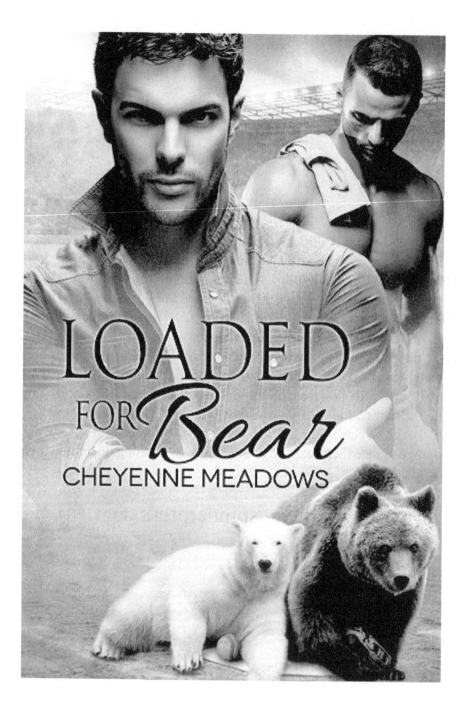

LOADED
FOR Bear
CHEYENNE MEADOWS

Shifter Hardball: Book Two

Polar bear shifter Graham Tundra can't believe his bad luck. Not only is he traded to another baseball team midseason, but he's also teamed up with Trigger Mallow: widely considered the best player in the game—but with the worst attitude.

Trigger is on the fence about Graham. As a grizzly bear shifter, he's relieved to have another ursine on the team, even if they are different species. The problem is Trigger is in the middle of his natural mating season, and Graham looks too damn good to pass up.

What begins as friends with benefits shows potential to grow into a deeper connection. If only they can put aside their differences, learn to trust, listen to their feelings, and realize it's more than just a bear thing.

www.dreamspinnerpress.com

FELINE
PERSUASION
CHEYENNE MEADOWS

When tiger shifter Cade turns an oily owner of a consultation firm over to the FBI, he finds himself with a hit man on his heels. Chester was in possession of security-breaching national secrets, and even more concerning, evidence that shifters exist, and if it got out, trouble would follow for all shifters. So now Cade is on the run. He holes up in an isolated hideout where he doesn't expect anyone to find him—least of all a former one-night stand.

Alpha lion shifter Micah can't shake Cade from his mind. They spent one glorious night together before Cade ran off without leaving even a name. He's determined to find his runaway and protect what he's come to think as his despite Cade's one and done rule. He surprises Cade in his secret nest in the forest, learns the reason for Cade's self-imposed exile, and decides to call for help. This nets them Stone: a top-of-the-line bodyguard and the one man Micah can't stand. Stone isn't thrilled either. He can think of better things to do than spend days in the wilderness with the uppity alpha who stomps on his last nerve.

Despite their differences and history, they need to find a way to survive and expose the traitor in their midst. They also realize chances at love are fleeting unless you grab the opportunity between your teeth and hold on for one wild ride.

www.dreamspinnerpress.com

CHEYENNE MEADOWS
RELENTLESS
The heart is relentless...
in both vengeance and love.

Jaguar shifter and sniper extraordinaire, Jag, is tasked with his most difficult and dangerous mission to date—take out the man responsible for his spotter and husband's violent death. Again.

Sonar, an ocelot shifter, is assigned as the new spotter to the surly and scowling feline alpha. He's impressed with Jag's skills but sees more beneath the surface: a grief-stricken and furious man on a trail of vengeance.

Together Sonar and Jag face perils and challenges that test their skills, resolve, and the budding feelings they have for each other. As the death toll rises, so does the heat between them. Their longings could give them the strength needed to persevere, but it also might force them to succumb and sacrifice everything. One thing's for certain: someone won't be making it back alive.

www.dreamspinnerpress.com

FOR **MORE** OF THE **BEST GAY ROMANCE**